ONE TRUE WISH

ONE TRUE WISH

Lauren Kate

Atheneum Books for Young Readers
New York London Toronto Sydney New Delhi

ATHENEUM BOOKS FOR YOUNG READERS

An imprint of Simon & Schuster Children's Publishing Division

1230 Avenue of the Americas, New York, New York 10020

ATHENEUM BOOKS FOR YOUNG READERS is a registered trademark of Simon & Schuster, Inc. Atheneum logo is a trademark of Simon & Schuster, Inc.

For information about special discounts for bulk purchases, please contact Simon & Schuster Special Sales at 1-866-506-1949 or business@simonandschuster.com.

The Simon & Schuster Speakers Bureau can bring authors to your live event. For more information or to book an event, contact the Simon & Schuster Speakers Bureau at 1-866-248-3049 or visit our website at www.simonspeakers.com.

Interior design by Irene Metaxatos.

The text for this book was set in Cormorant Garamond.

Manufactured in the United States of America

0323 FFG

First Edition

10 9 8 7 6 5 4 3 2 1

Library of Congress Cataloging-in-Publication Data

Names: Kate, Lauren, author.

Title: One true wish / Lauren Kate.

Description: First edition. | New York : Atheneum Books for Young Readers, 2023. | Audience: Ages 10 and Up. | Summary: Phoebe is a wish-granting fairy who does not believe in children, so when she crash-lands in the woods, she is surprised to meet three twelve-year-olds who could use a true wish, but first they must race against the clock to restore Phoebe's powers and get her back home.

Identifiers: LCCN 2022004255

ISBN 9781665910569 (hardcover) | ISBN 9781665910583 (ebook)

Subjects: LCSH: Fairies—Juvenile fiction. | Wishes—Juvenile fiction. | Magic—Juvenile fiction. | Gender-nonconforming children—Juvenile fiction. | Best friends—Juvenile fiction. | Friendship—Juvenile fiction. | Texas—Juvenile fiction. | CYAC: Fairies—Fiction. | Wishes—Fiction. | Magic—Fiction. | Gender identity—Fiction. | Best friends—Fiction. | Friendship—Fiction.

Classification: LCC PZ7.K15655 On 2023 | DDC 813.6 [Fic]--dc23/eng/20220531

LC record available at https://lccn.loc.gov/2022004255

For Kris
1974-2020

❋

"... all the stars
which long were pressed and hidden in the mass,
began to gleam out from the plains of heaven ..."
—*The Metamorphoses*

ONE TRUE WISH

ONE

Birdie

Birdie Borovsky had been waiting for this day for years. But on the afternoon the fairy landed, practically in her best friend Gem's front yard, Birdie didn't even feel the quake. She was distracted by the scene unfolding in Gem's kitchen.

"I WISH I'D NEVER BEEN BORN!"

Lately her best friend screamed. A lot. Sometimes out of nowhere.

"Gemima Cash, what an awful thing to say!" Mrs. Cash was an accountant and still in her work clothes, though she'd taken off her heels. "And over a piece of cantaloupe? You'll have some, Birdie, won't you?" She was holding out the cutting board, really not reading the room.

It wasn't Mrs. Cash's fault. All she'd done was slice some fruit on one of those cutting boards that looked like the cross section of a tree. The cutting boards in Birdie's house were plastic and flimsy as a fingernail. They made everything taste like onions. Gem's mom wasn't anything like Birdie's mom, which was one reason Birdie spent so much time at Gem's house.

Birdie appreciated the effort Mrs. Cash took to stick a toothpick into the center of each cold cube of cantaloupe. Still, out of solidarity, there was no chance Birdie could accept. She was on thin ice with Gem already, simply for having mentioned she was starving, that she hadn't hardly eaten lunch. Which was true. But it was the wrong thing to say. It made Gem look at Birdie like she was a real idiot, like anyone with one brain cell should know that the topic of *lunch* was forbidden.

To be honest, Birdie probably should have known.

"*No one* understands me," Gem fumed, even though Birdie was trying to do just that. For the whole second half of sixth grade, understanding Gem was a lot like algebra: the harder Birdie tried, the worse she did.

She knew it had started at lunch. She knew it had to do with Felix Howard. She knew—everyone knew—Felix Howard was the worst. What she didn't know was how to help Gem feel better. Because the things that happened to Gem didn't happen to Birdie.

Like: Felix Howard backing up on purpose in the cafeteria line and elbowing Gem in the boob. Then saying, loud enough for everyone to hear, that he was hungry for some melons. Birdie had felt her temperature rise, along with a few curse words she would have loved to sling at Felix. But then Birdie looked at Gem.

A weird thing about sixth grade was that there were moments when you didn't recognize your best friend. A year ago, Gem would have punched Felix Howard. But a year ago, Gem didn't have boobs.

Maybe boobs made all the difference. Birdie wouldn't know.

Gem didn't even look at Felix Howard. Even when he ended his taunt with one of his signature, thunderous, disgusting burps. She just walked past him with her tray and didn't say a word about it, even to Birdie, the rest of lunch. When Birdie called Felix Howard a pig, Gem snapped at Birdie and said she didn't want to talk about it. Worse, she'd turned away from Birdie, to Ava Rhodes at the other end of the table, and started talking about their history dioramas, due on Friday. It was like Gem just swallowed what had happened.

Right until the moment her mom put the cutting board of cantaloupe on the table.

"You used to love melon," Mrs. Cash said. "Remember

that honeydew sorbet I made last Fourth of July?"

Gem's pencil tip snapped against her paper in the middle of her "Parts of a Whole" essay.

If Mrs. Cash had looked at her daughter then, she would have seen it: that moment just before the rowboat goes over the edge of the waterfall. She would have dumped the cantaloupe down the garbage disposal, no questions asked. She used to be good at stuff like that. She was one of those moms you felt was on a kid's side. But she was halfway inside the refrigerator by then and muttering about expiration dates on yogurt.

Birdie closed the notebook where she'd been working on her comic for the final issue of the school newspaper. She readied herself for whatever would come.

"I HATE cantaloupe, and I HATE you!" Gem screamed. Then she flung her chair back and pushed the whole cutting board off the table, until there was cantaloupe everywhere, even in the dog bowl, and a pale pool of juice was oozing toward Mrs. Cash's pedicure.

Gem bolted for the side door. She let it slam behind her. She hadn't taken Birdie with her.

Birdie wished Gem had bothered to look back, to say with her eyes, *C'mon. I need you, my best friend.* Instead the kitchen filled up with the awful quiet of Gem not being there.

Even though Mrs. Cash probably didn't expect Birdie

to stay and help clean up, Birdie still felt bad when she went running after Gem. She had to. That's what best friends did.

But as she jogged out into the humid Texas afternoon, Birdie had a funny feeling that something wasn't right. Something bigger than Gem's mood. Something bigger even than Gem and Birdie's friendship. Something in the air.

Something she'd forgotten she'd been waiting for.

Two

Van

One minute, Van was sitting alone in their da's kitchen, avoiding their English essay and binging Birdie B's comic archive on their phone. The next minute, out of nowhere, the house shook, and a deep *boom* sounded close by.

Van was the only one downstairs. There was no way they were going upstairs to ask their da's girlfriend, Nirusha, whether she'd felt it too. They put down their phone and ran outside. The sound rang in the air.

After a moment, their ears picked up something else: a thrashing coming from the woods. They stood on their da's diving board and looked out at the slope of dirt beyond the fence, at the stand of trees beyond that. The sun hung over a canopy of leaves. It would be dark in an hour.

Van had never explored these woods before. When they stayed at their da's, they boycotted everything that pre-divorce Van would have thought was fun. Van wanted their da to see how miserable they were, how miserable he'd made them. So far, he hadn't picked up on their hints.

It had been more than a year since Van moved to Texas from Ireland, but people still called them "the new kid." Even though there were a dozen *newer* students who started at Wonder Middle at the beginning of sixth grade. When Van cried about this at night to their mam, convinced that they were weird and not in a good way, their mam insisted that they simply hadn't "found their people yet."

Van used to have people. They used to have parents who were married, and a house so close to the shore they could walk there without shoes. They didn't like to think about their life in Ireland. It felt so distant that it seemed more like it had happened to a character in a show.

Van had braces, glasses, big feet, sad eyes. They'd gotten a short haircut at the beginning of sixth grade, and it was a mistake. They didn't look like Josie Totah. They looked like someone with enormous earlobes. They'd developed a tick of tugging on their hair, as if they could make it grow faster.

They hopped off the diving board and walked to their

da's back gate. Heading for the woods, Van wasn't scared, only curious. It seemed like something had landed out there, and now that something was in trouble. A hawk? An owl? In Ireland, Van might have recognized the sound as any number of native birds, but here, they didn't know.

The thrashing made it easy for Van to track. And soon they heard another sound, a faint tinkling, like a bell. Something about that sound . . . It made Van wish their best friend Caro was at their side. But Caro was twelve hours away by plane. Far enough that their old friendship wasn't worth wishing for anymore. It had been a long time since Van even let themself think about the easy fun they used to have back home.

Alone was what Van was now. So alone Van went into the woods.

They came to an elm tree, whose exposed roots jutted up around its trunk like the arms of a star. The roots were gnarled and thick, almost as tall as Van. The sound was coming from the other side. They propped their elbows on the elm roots and peered over. For several moments, they couldn't get their mind around what they were seeing.

A creature lay faceup, twitching in a pile of leaves. It was much smaller than Van, about the size of a new baby, but its face was mature, fine-featured, with a long nose and pointed chin. Its face made it look like it was Van's age, twelve. It wore a shiny green dress of unusual fabric and had tangled red hair splayed out in all directions. Its belly could best be described as pot.

Van thought back to the comic they'd just been reading on their phone. The thing in the leaves looked a *little* like Phoebe LaCroix—the cheeky, eponymous villain from Birdie B's weekly comic strip, who lived on a distant star.

"No way," Van whispered. They swiped off their glasses, cleaned them on their sleeve, and set them back on their nose. The sight before them stayed the same.

Now the creature twitched toward Van, turning its head and widening its golden eyes. In its gaze, Van saw fear so sharp and real it reached out and pricked them.

"Are you hurt?" Van asked.

They'd left their phone on their da's counter. Should they run back to the house and call 911? But they didn't want to leave the creature, not even for a moment.

In the time it took Van to climb over the roots, the creature had struggled to its feet. Facing Van, pointy chin jutting up, it smashed a crimson flower-petal hat back atop its head. Only then did Van notice two dusty gray wings extending from its back.

"You're seeing things," Van told themself under their breath. A couple of years ago, this thought wouldn't have occurred to them. In Ireland, children were raised on a diet of fairy lore, and there were reasonable people—like

Van's very own Gran—who actually believed. When their parents separated, Van's first instinct had been to go to the fairy hill near their aunt's and make offerings, begging the fairies to put their parents back together. By the time the divorce was final, things were different. Van was different. They'd returned to the hill and destroyed their offerings. They had sworn off fairies.

So this thing could not be a fairy, because Van did not believe in fairies.

They closed their eyes. "Count to three. When you open your eyes, it'll be gone."

But when Van opened their eyes, not only had the not-fairy not disappeared, it did the last thing Van expected. It let out an enormous burp. The sound vibrated, shaking the trees.

The creature's cheeks turned pink. It placed a delicate hand over its mouth.

"Whoa," Van said, fighting back an urge to laugh.

It pointed with a trembling arm. "What *are* you?"

"Me?" Van blinked. They touched their chest. "I'm a . . . human?"

"As in, a human-*Child*?" the creature asked, crossing its arms.

"Yeah, I guess, technically," Van said. They'd finally gotten their da to stop calling them a *young woman*, but *human-child* didn't feel exactly right either.

"Ha!" The creature stamped its foot. "Children don't exist."

When Van laughed, the creature walked a circle around them, squinting crossly. Beneath its torn gown . . . webbed feet poked out. Another feature of Phoebe LaCroix in Birdie B's comic strip. This was getting weird.

"Are you a puppet?" it asked Van. "Did the priestess stitch you for a solstice play? Why is it so cold on this moon, and *what* is wrong with my wings?" The creature swatted at them angrily.

"What are *you*?" Van asked.

The creature placed a hand over its chest. "I am Phoebe, Fairy of the North Star."

"No. No, you're not." Van rubbed their eyes. Were they that lonely that they'd resorted to imagining friends out of comic strips? "That's impossible. You're . . . made-up."

The creature hooted with laughter. "You don't believe *me*? That's rich!"

"Okay," Van said. "Prove you're a fairy."

"Prove *you're* a Child!" the creature shot back.

"How would I prove I'm a child?" Van said. It was the craziest thing they'd ever heard.

The creature that called herself Phoebe tilted her head and smirked. "Make a wish."

THREE

Birdie

Birdie jogged toward the street. She knew where Gem had gone. Gem's house was at the end of a cul-de-sac, except instead of the circle being filled only with concrete, whoever built this street left these two old crabapple trees in the center and paved the road around them.

Over the years, a tall border of holly bushes, spindly ivies, and Mexican feather grass had grown up on that patch of earth around the crabapple trees. It was a little wilderness in the middle of the street. It looked more impenetrable than it was, and Birdie and Gem knew the best places to crawl through. They knew which branches to climb so you could see out but not be seen. On days like today, when the crabapples were blooming, Birdie felt like she was disappearing into a hot pink jungle on another planet when she slipped inside.

This was the one place where she and Gem could make the world the way they liked it. In the crabapples, Gem was an astronaut at SpaceX, and Birdie was a journalist, speaking truth to power, like her idol, Katy Tur. They were both important. Not just to relatives, but to the wider world. Even if it was just for an hour before dinner, until Gem's mom called them down and Birdie biked the three miles back to her apartment. For a little while each afternoon, they were *something*.

But today Gem wasn't there.

Instead Birdie found Gem's little brother, Marley, at the crabapples, arranging some sticks at the base of one of the tree trunks.

"What are *you* doing here?" Birdie asked.

Marley didn't look up. "Making a nest."

Birdie noticed the subtle outlines of Darth Vader all over the fabric of his T-shirt, which was kind of cool and kind of dorky and just so incredibly Marley to straddle that line. Marley was only a year younger than Birdie, but the difference between them felt bigger. She couldn't remember the last time she'd hung out with him.

"A nest for what?" she said.

"I'll know soon."

Birdie rolled her eyes. Marley was bizarre. "Gem told you not to play here. Remember?"

"Did you feel the earthquake?" Marley asked.

"Huh?" There weren't earthquakes in Wichita Falls.

Marley looked at her then. He had crystal-blue eyes, nothing like Gem's deep brown pools, and his skin was several shades lighter than Gem's, but it was amazing how much brother and sister looked alike, all their features the same shape. Both Cash kids had very curly hair in a shiny shade of brown. They had thick, arched eyebrows, dark lashes, and particularly nice teeth.

Birdie was okay in the looks department, but she felt like everything had to be going right for it to show. Like the weather couldn't be too humid, and she couldn't be wearing orange or have forgotten to put on sunscreen the day before. Birdie was in a battle against her freckles: enough was enough.

"I heard her run off toward the woods," Marley said.

Birdie would never have thought to look in the woods. Had Gem not come to the crabapples because she didn't want Birdie to find her? "Did she know *you* were in here?" she asked Marley. That might explain it.

He shrugged. "Why's she so mad? Felix Howard?"

Birdie squinted at him. "What do you know about Felix Howard?"

"I heard he was a jerk to her at lunch."

"Yeah, well." Birdie didn't know what to say about that. It wasn't exactly good news that the incident made its way not just to the Lower School, but to its outsiders, to Marley. And Birdie definitely didn't want to talk about Gem's boobs with Marley. The thought made her itch.

"I'm gonna go find her," Birdie said, nodding at Marley's stick pile. "You're not about to set anything on fire, are you?"

He laughed like he felt sorry for Birdie that she'd thought something so dumb. "That was *one* time, when I was five. You think people stay the same their whole lives, don't you?"

"No," Birdie said. She wasn't sure why the comment nagged at her. People changed. Obviously. For example: Gem.

Gem used to be . . .

Gem wasn't always so . . .

Gem used to *like* Birdie.

Was it that pathetically simple? Birdie was surprised to feel she might cry. Since the start of May, as the other kids counted down the days until school let out for summer—eight—Birdie's anxiety counted up. What was so great about summer? *Nothing* was the answer, if you were Birdie.

For the past three years, Gem had spent her summers at a super-fun sleepaway camp that Birdie's family couldn't afford. She was gone for six weeks, and Birdie was lucky to get six letters. This year, Birdie worried she might not even get one of those fill-in-the-blanks camp postcards.

It was always weird for a few days after Gem came home from camp. When the two of them would start talking at the same time ("Go ahead," "No, you first") and could never agree on anything that sounded fun enough to do. This year, Birdie didn't know if their friendship could survive that awkward phase. And if it didn't?

What would it be like to start seventh grade without a best friend? Birdie guessed she'd have all summer to worry about that.

"You know where the creek is?" Marley asked. "I bet she's there."

Birdie nodded. She sort of did.

"Need my help?" Marley asked.

"Why would I need your help?" Birdie snapped. She didn't mean to sound so annoyed. None of this was Marley's fault. Birdie couldn't think of anyone to blame, except Felix Howard, which didn't do her any good. She needed to find Gem.

"Because you're still standing here," Marley said.

"Not for long." Birdie sniffed and trudged off.

FOUR

Van

Okay, I did it," Van said. "I made a wish. Now what?"

"Where is it?" Phoebe said, looking around.

"Where is . . . what?"

"Your wish." She paced the elm tree roots, agitated. "I don't see it anywhere."

"How would you *see* a wish?" Van asked.

"Little, golden, wriggly thing?" Phoebe said, like Van was dense. "The kind I've been fishing out of my Wishwell for thousands of years? You are really not convincing as a Child. Next time you play at this, you should try to be a little more awesome."

"Awesome?"

"Yes, awesome. And all-knowing. And desiring only what you truly need. For that is what makes a Child."

"Er, not the ones that I know," Van said, and they stared at each other until Phoebe's face twitched and she stuck out her tongue.

"If you don't believe I'm a child," Van said, "what exactly do you think I am?"

They really wanted to know.

"Whatever you are," Phoebe said, "it's *your* problem. I'd guess you're some giant breed of fairy working for the priestess. I'd guess she put you up to this whole charade."

"Why would someone do that?"

"To convince fair folk like me to *believe*."

"In what?"

"In the *Children Tale*!" Phoebe cried, poking a finger at Van's shin. "Now, tell me what the priestess does with all those granted wishes. Hoards them for herself, does she?"

"I . . . really wouldn't know," Van said. "You think someone's out there stealing wishes?" If this were true, it might explain a few things.

"The wish you claim you made seems to have conveniently disappeared," Phoebe said. "What'd you wish for, anyway?"

"I thought I wasn't supposed to tell anyone," Van said, sitting down with their back against the tree trunk, watching Phoebe flit back and forth. "Or else it won't come true?"

"Whoever told you that?"

"Everyone?"

"This is hocus-pocus," Phoebe said, and marched off toward the tree roots, which she began, with difficulty, to climb. "I won't fall for it. Because I know the *Children Tale* is make-believe. I'm going home, and I'm going to tell everyone about the impostors posing as Children on this moon! Acting boring! Spreading lies!"

Van looked around the woods. Wishwells? Impostor Children? What was happening? This creature who claimed to be a wish-granting fairy was acting like *Van* was the apparition. Van found themself losing their patience.

"If you really can grant wishes, then why didn't you help me when I needed you?" The question flew from their mouth before they could stop it. Van was horrified. They clamped their lips shut and rode out the flame in their cheeks.

"Why would I help *you*?" the creature asked, abandoning the tree roots and spinning to face Van. "I serve *Children*. Or I did, back when I was fool enough to believe in them. You clearly don't even know how to make a wish."

"I wished for a puppy, all right?!" Van said. It was the first thing that popped into their mind. They still had a paper due tomorrow, and *I met a fairy in the woods* was probably not going to fly as an excuse for turning it in late.

"What's a puppy?" Phoebe asked.

Van threw up their hands. "See, I knew you weren't a

wish fairy. If you were, you would have granted about ten trillion wishes for puppies."

"Let's not get mired in specifics," Phoebe said. "Everyone knows fairies see the essence of wishes over the details. The way one sees in darkness—outlines, shadows, et cetera."

"This is not real," Van said to themself. "Your imagination is playing tricks on you because you're lonely. If you leave now, if you go back to Da's and write your paper, practice your flute, you can pretend this never happened."

"Wait a minute." Phoebe hopped onto Van's knee, and the very real weight of her, webbed feet on Van's bare knee, made Van suck in their breath.

"Was it a true wish?" Phoebe asked.

"What?"

"As the Child Eriopis once said: 'There's a difference between a true wish and a passing desire. A true wish can't be outgrown. A true wish grows with you.'" She stopped talking suddenly, as if she feared she'd said too much. She glared at Van and slid backward off their knee. "If you were a Child, you'd know that."

This struck Van more than they expected. They had no idea who the Child Eriopis was; still, they understood what Phoebe meant. A puppy would be fun, but there were things Van wished for more. Trouble was, those things were buried so deep within them, Van didn't know if they could put them into words.

In the space of a few seconds, Van had gone from dismissing Phoebe to wondering . . . What if Van humored this figment of their imagination? Where would the conversation go?

"How'd you end up in Texas?" they asked.

"I'm not in Texas!" Phoebe laughed. "I can clearly see that this is a moon designed to make me *think* I'm in Texas. To make me feel exiled and sorry for ruining everything. And I am. Sorry. I would like to return to Polaris now. To my hut. I'm tired, and very, very cold."

Van wiped sweat off their brow. It was ninety degrees in the shade and not even summer yet. "I'd like to go home too. But unfortunately, Texas is where we both are."

"No," Phoebe said. "All the literature says fairies *don't* leave the North Star system. I wouldn't have survived the journey. My wings would be in tatters!" She spread her tattered wings.

In Birdie B's comic, Phoebe LaCroix had much nicer wings than these. Van didn't know why their imagination would have invented such busted wings.

"Are they always so . . . *gray?*" they asked.

"My wings are not gray! They're positively luminescent. Perhaps your eyes aren't capable of registering my variegations—" Then suddenly Phoebe broke off, looked over her shoulder, and let out an earsplitting scream.

FIVE

Birdie

Birdie heard the scream from the woods.

Gem.

She started running toward the sound. She cut between the Barons' yard and some old people's whose names she didn't know. She turned sideways to slip through a narrow part, dodging half-dead rose thorns along the fence that led to the alley.

The only time Birdie could remember coming back here was for her wildflower project in third grade, when they had to pick and press and categorize fifty different Texas wildflowers. It took Birdie months, way after the due date, probably because both of her parents refused to help. Mrs. Cash finally took pity on Birdie and brought her out here to find the last few flowers.

Birdie made herself think about wildflowers. Instead of something terrible happening to Gem in the woods. Indian blanket. Verbena. Texas winecup.

If something had happened to Gem, Birdie didn't know what she would do. They'd been best friends since they were three years old and met at the dentist's office. Gem had been crying, their moms started talking, the rest was history.

On the other side of the alley, Birdie entered a thicket of elms and oaks. Soon the world got dimmer, a little cooler, and suddenly Birdie could smell the woods. Like someone had stuck a scratch-and-sniff sticker called *woods* under her nose.

She hurried down a slope of crunchy leaves. Around a big boulder. More trees. She heard water. The creek! What if Gem had fallen in? Birdie ran.

Indian blanket. Verbena. Texas winecup.

And then, her heart lifted as the creek came into view, and she saw Gem standing on the other side.

Her best friend looked . . . fine. Maybe Birdie hadn't heard what she thought she'd heard. The view of Gem, safe and whole, held Birdie in a grateful trance. There was something about the way Gem moved and talked and did little things like adjust one ringlet of her hair that made people look and keep looking. Teachers liked her on the first day of school. Strangers talked to her at restaurants. Even Tom Ng, the lifeguard at the community pool, knew Gem's name. Birdie was proud to have a best friend like Gem. When they were together, she felt shielded from the rest of the world.

Gem's eyes were scanning the creek bed, like she was searching for stones to skip. She looked so peaceful, so unlike she had looked the last time Birdie saw her. Birdie wanted to leave Gem in that place where all that mattered was finding a good stone to skip, where she wasn't thinking about school, or screaming at her mom, or any kind of melon.

At the same time, Birdie also wanted Gem to know she'd come. That she would always come for her friend.

"Gem."

Gem looked up. Her features pinched. "Hey."

"Did you hear something?" Birdie asked. "A scream?"

Gem shrugged. "I don't know."

"It was loud," Birdie said. "I thought something happened."

"Did my mom send you?" Gem asked. "How long am I grounded for?"

Whose side did Gem think Birdie was on? Anyway, Gem's mom wasn't even mean like that. Birdie crossed the creek, trying to hop along the rocks. Her shoes got soaked.

"I've been thinking. Felix Howard shouldn't get away with—"

"It's not like you can do anything about it," Gem cut her off. She seemed annoyed at Birdie as she turned and started walking deeper into the woods.

Birdie had just about caught up to Gem when the two of them ran smack into the new kid, Van Falls.

SIX

Van

It was almost funny. All year Van had admired Birdie B, who sat in front of them in science and created the comic strip that was Van's favorite thing about school. The comic strip whose villain was possibly, at this very moment, magically incarnate on the other side of the elm roots. But this was not the time to fankid. Van needed more time to get to the bottom of this Phoebe situation. Alone.

"Er—" they said. "Could you . . . please . . ."

And they were blowing it.

"Are you okay, Van?" Birdie asked.

"Just leave me alone!" Van shrieked.

They wished there was a world where this wasn't the

first complete sentence they ever said to Birdie B. But then there might not be *this* world, in which something potentially magical was happening, and Van was the one it was happening to.

A true wish, Phoebe had said. Van knew it wasn't possible. But it was so tempting to wonder what if. What would Van's life be like if wishes could come true?

No, they'd made that mistake before. The mistake of believing. And what did they have to show for it? Divorced parents and a chronic case of homesickness.

"Ahem," Phoebe said from behind the tree roots.

"What was that?" Birdie asked, like a dog who'd just caught whiff of an interesting scent.

Wait, had Birdie heard Phoebe's voice? Was Van possibly *not* imagining things? That would be even more bizarre. Then again, Van had to admit that being confronted by Birdie and her friend—these two totally ordinary kids—drove home the sheer *extra*ordinariness of Phoebe.

Their heart was pounding. What should they do? Their eyes flicked to the right, where, over their shoulder, Phoebe was probably still trying to use her broken wings.

"Fine, we'll leave you alone," Birdie's friend said. Her name was Gem, and Van barely knew her, but they could tell from the way she carried her shoulders that she was a little hung up on herself. "We didn't even know you were here."

"I'm *not* here," Van said. They looked at Birdie. Birdie was going to be their problem. Birdie was curious.

Go, Van tried to convince them with their mind. And a few seconds later, Gem nodded and turned on her heel.

"See ya," she called.

"Hold on." Birdie caught Gem's arm before Van had a chance to feel relieved. "We're not leaving yet."

Van's stomach twisted. They stuffed their hands in the pockets of their jumpsuit and tried not to show their nerves. Van had stopped wearing this jumpsuit in public the first week of school, when Felix Howard said Van looked like a car mechanic. It was so comfortable, and everyone Van knew in Ireland wore them, but everyone Van knew in Ireland was also totally fine with them being nonbinary. Here, it was so different. More precisely, Van was so different. And in this town, different wasn't a good thing.

Deep in their pocket, Van's fingers grazed something cool to the touch. They closed it in their palm and remembered. It was one of the darts from the board in Caro's basement. The favorite pastime of Van and their old best friend. Caro had included it in Van's going-away present, and Van used to carry it everywhere. But when they'd stopped wearing this jumpsuit, they'd forgotten they'd left the dart in it. If Caro were here, Van would have someone to share Phoebe with. Someone they trusted. Unlike these kids. Van missed their friend with a force they hadn't let themself feel in a while.

"Fine then, *I'll* leave," Van bluffed, praying Birdie wouldn't follow them back over the other side of the roots. But why would Birdie follow Van? She was here with her friend. She and Gem didn't want anything to do with Van.

"You live near here?" Birdie asked.

Van stood still and nodded at the neighborhood on the far side of the woods where they lived half the week with their da. It was called Oak Bluff. All the houses had pools, Van's da had bragged when they'd first moved in. But why would Van care if someone else's house had a pool? Van barely swam in their da's pool. They preferred the ocean. The nearest ocean was a seven-hour drive away. They'd told that to their da.

Because the point was to get rid of these kids, Van didn't mention to Birdie that the other half of the week they lived with their mam in a tiny old rental house whose stained ceilings they'd covered with brightly patterned scarves, and it was right across the street from the apartment complex where Van knew Birdie lived.

If Birdie had seen Van biking to school even half as much as Van had seen Birdie biking to school, she didn't mention it.

"You come here a lot?" Birdie asked.

This got Van tangled up. If they said yes, what if these

kids also came here a lot? Birdie would know Van was lying. If Van told the truth, that they'd never set foot in these woods before today, then Birdie might ask why they had come.

"None of your business," Van said crisply. "You're always so nosy, Birdie."

They didn't know why they'd said that. They didn't mean it. They liked Birdie, even wanted to be friends with Birdie. But then, the kids you wanted to be friends with were the most dangerous sort. Because they might make you drop your guard. And then they could hurt you. Van didn't drop their guard for anyone.

Birdie was staring at them, hands on her hips. "Maybe I am nosy, but you're being sus."

"I am not," Van insisted. They were sweating again. Totally sus.

"What's back there?" Birdie asked. "Why do you keep looking over your shoulder?" She leaned to the right, to Van's left. She stood on her toes and raised her chin.

"Stop it," Van said.

When Birdie didn't stop, and instead tried to move past, Van launched to tackle the girl in an awkward piggyback. One of their arms came around Birdie's neck, the other over her eyes. Van could not believe what they were doing. They also couldn't stop. Anything to prevent Birdie from making it to the far side of the roots.

"Let go of me!" Birdie clawed at Van, spun around in circles. No one besides Van's mam had been this close to Van since they moved to Texas, and Van was very aware of every place the two of them were touching. Birdie bashed Van's back against the rough bark of the tree.

"Ow!" Van yelped as Birdie tripped over her feet and both kids thudded to the ground.

Now Birdie's friend Gem was involved, trying to pry Van's arms apart. Van struggled, outnumbered, until finally they lost their grip. A second later, Birdie was dashing to the top of the tree roots.

Gem looked down at Van. She did the last thing Van expected. She put out a hand to help them up. Van took it, for efficiency, then scrambled after Birdie.

"You don't see it. You don't see it," Van muttered under their breath at Birdie's back. "Please tell me you don't see it."

Birdie spun on Van, eyes wild. She looked . . . scared. "Is this your idea of a joke?"

SEVEN

Gem

When Gem first laid eyes on the creature, she felt something lift in her she hadn't known had a weight. She felt like she was a balloon at a birthday party that someone had let go of.

She used to be into magic—unicorns and mermaids, leprechauns and a whole Harry Potter phase—but she was in sixth grade now, almost seventh. Reality had set in several years ago. And yet, here this was. So definitely *not* human. So real. Tears filled Gem's eyes. No one had to explain this to her. Her intuition told her simply to believe. She hopped down from the roots to study the creature. The gauzy gray wings, a little worse for wear. Lovely eyelashes, cute nose. There was a fairy in their midst. "Wow."

"You can see her?" Van said. "Both of you actually *see* her?"

"Who put you up to this, Van?" Birdie said, her voice a little shaky.

"No one! I didn't—I just—I heard the sound, I came out here and—"

"Who are *they*?" the fairy demanded, springy with panic. She pointed at Birdie and Gem. "More impostors!"

Impostors? Gem looked to Van for help. The only thing she knew about the new kid was that they went by *they*. Now she knew something else: the lengths to which this kid had gone to hide the creature from them. Would Gem have done the same? Would she have tried to keep something this miraculous a secret? Even from Birdie?

"She doesn't believe in children," Van explained.

Gem laughed. Actually laughed. All day, she'd thought nothing could stop Felix Howard's awful joke from looping on repeat through her mind. She'd thought nothing could shake her out of her humiliation. But this did shake her. This moved her. Out of her own body almost completely. Looking at the creature, Gem could forget herself, which was what she really wanted to do. Here was a fairy who didn't believe in kids. It was funny.

"Where'd you come from?" Gem asked the fairy.

"Someone planted her here," Birdie said darkly,

thrumming her fingers against her chin. "Someone with a sick mind and a crude sense of robotics. Someone who knew I'd be passing through the woods today—"

"Birdie," Gem said. "This is not a robot. This is real. She's alive. Can't you see that—"

"AI can do all sorts of stuff these days," Birdie cut her off. She wasn't looking at the fairy. She was pacing the roots of the tree. "You can buy this junk on Amazon. And when I find out who did, even if it's Felix Howard . . . *especially* if it's Felix Howard . . . I'll—"

"You're being paranoid," Gem said. She wanted to sit down with the fairy and see what she could do. She wanted the fairy to know she wouldn't hurt her, and that even if the fairy didn't believe in children, Gem believed in her.

"How'd she get here?" Gem asked Van.

"Did either of you feel the quake?" Van said.

Gem shook her head.

"I think she made it," Van whispered. "I think she . . . fell."

"Fell from *where*?" Gem said. They all looked up at the trees for a while.

After a stretch of quiet, Van said, "The North Star?"

No one laughed, which was bizarre to Gem. Recently it felt like you could get laughed at for walking too slow, or not slow enough, for knowing the answer when you got called on in math, or for not knowing the answer. It felt like you could get laughed at for breathing weird. Hadn't Gem laughed at other kids this year for the littlest things, mostly so that someone else would be the object of the laughter, and Gem would be spared for a few moments?

But no one laughed now because, as wild as Van's answer was, it also might be true.

"I'm not saying I believe it," Van explained. "It's just what she said."

"I definitely don't believe it," Birdie said.

"I mean, if fairies could grant wishes," Van said, "life wouldn't be the way it is."

"Exactly," Birdie said.

"Take me home!" the fairy wailed. "I don't like this moon, and I don't like this play. It's dull and doesn't make sense. I'll be good. I won't tell anyone it's all a lie. Just take me home!"

"Phoebe?" Van said softly.

"Wait, why did you call her that?" Birdie asked, a high note of doubt in her voice.

Birdie had used this same skeptical tone the night Gem confided she'd gotten her period. Birdie had thought Gem was joking, so Gem had pretended she *was* joking. She never mentioned it again until Birdie saw the box of pads in her bathroom two months later, and Gem had to tell her all over again. It was awful. It was one of a few reasons why Gem felt like she couldn't talk to Birdie anymore.

Not about the real things that she most needed to say. She didn't have anyone she could say those things to.

"She told me her name," Van said.

"What else did she tell you?" Gem asked.

Van hesitated, and Gem got it. The new kid had discovered the fairy, and now they were being forced to share her with two strangers. Gem wouldn't be happy about that either.

"Van?" Birdie urged.

Van's mouth twitched, and then it all came rushing out, like they wanted to stop it but couldn't. "She told me she came from the North Star. She told me she grants wishes. Or she used to, before she stopped believing in kids. She says there's some priestess who made up the story of children, and who's stealing the wishes Phoebe used to grant."

A shiver passed through Gem. "Wow."

"Y'all believe that?" Birdie said. "The North Star is a giant ball of gas. It's, like, uninhabitable."

"It's far nicer than this ice sheet," Phoebe shot back. She was trying to climb the tree roots, trying to get away. "Where's the river on this moon? If I can't fly, I'll swim home."

"Someone's playing a prank on me," Birdie said, crossing her arms over her chest.

"Birdie, what does this have to do with *you*?" Gem asked, exasperated.

Birdie gaped at Gem. Her mouth was open, but no words came out. Which was unusual for Birdie.

"Why are you looking at me like that?" Gem asked.

"Do you even *read* my comic?" Birdie sounded crushed.

"Your comic?" Gem said. She didn't want to admit that she'd stopped reading the *Wonder Gazette* months ago because it made her feel like a freak. The articles—"Spotlight on Honor Roller Trudy Higginbottom!"—made Gem feel like every other kid at Wonder was constantly living their best life, and Gem was the only one for whom school was a daily form of torture. It was nothing against Birdie or her obvious creative talent. Gem's boycott was a small act of self-care. And she really didn't see what it had to do with the situation at hand.

"The similarities *are* astonishing," Van said to Birdie, just as Phoebe, who'd been trying to climb the tree roots, slipped and tumbled backward into a pile of leaves.

"Owwww."

Gem bent to help the fairy, who'd landed wrong on her sad-looking wings.

"Stay back, Impostor!" The fairy scrambled away like Gem was dangerous. Picking leaves ferociously out of her tangled red hair, Phoebe muttered to herself: "One skeptical bone in your body, and look where it gets you!"

"That is literally out of a panel in my comic," Birdie said, incredulous.

"*She was born with a skeptical bone in her body. It was in her left big toe,*" Van said, and Gem realized they must be quoting something Birdie had written. Gem scrolled back through her memory, and yeah, she did recall a character named Phoebe in Birdie's comic strip. Still:

She lowered her voice and turned to Birdie. "I think this is bigger than some comic."

Birdie closed her eyes and turned away, like Gem had just given her a terminal diagnosis.

Gem would deal with her friend's drama later. Right now, they had to make a plan about Phoebe. "What do you need?" Gem asked the fairy. "We can help you."

"I wouldn't say no to a cup of stardust tea! Two parts stardust, eight parts honey." She sounded delirious, staring into the trees and wagging a tiny finger. "Don't forget the honey."

"We're fresh out of stardust," Birdie said sarcastically.

When Birdie's feelings were hurt, she got snarky like this, which made it hard for Gem to apologize, which made their arguments stretch on.

"I mean, technically, we're made of stardust," Van said.

"You going to boil yourself up, Van?" Birdie said.

Van's cheeks flushed. They didn't answer. Gem wanted to tell Van not to take it personally; it was Gem who Birdie was mad at. It was Gem who hadn't read Birdie's comics.

"We can make you tea," Gem said to Phoebe.

"No," Birdie said, spinning around, surprising Gem with her open panic. "We can't. We won't. This is a trick—"

"She's lost," Gem said, "and afraid. And there's something wrong with her wings." What Gem didn't say aloud was that if she could pour her energy into helping Phoebe, then she might not have any energy left over to hate herself, at least for a little while. "I'm Gem. This is Birdie."

"Birdie." Phoebe tested out the name.

"But I guess you already knew that, right?" Birdie said.

"They're children," Van chimed in. "Real, live children. Just like me."

"Nope." The fairy shook her head. "Negatory."

"She thinks we're supposed to be more awesome," Van said.

Gem considered this. The fairy had a point. She crouched and put out her hand. "Nice to meet you, Phoebe."

The fairy squinted, then leaned forward and gave Gem's pinkie finger a sniff. Gem felt a tug on her thumbnail, and then the fairy landed on the back of her hand. A moment later, with exceedingly light steps, Phoebe was running up the length of Gem's arm. She reached Gem's neck, then hoisted herself higher, climbing up Gem's ear. She stopped atop Gem's head.

"*You*," Phoebe said.

"What about me?" Gem said, breathless.

With tiny fingers, Phoebe started combing through

Gem's hair. Her touch was cold, strange in the humid Texas afternoon. Gem tried to stay still as the fairy's fingers trailed down her face. Phoebe examined behind Gem's ears. She checked her fingernails again, then took off one of Gem's shoes and looked between her toes. She gave Gem's foot a sniff. "Hmmm."

"What is it?" Gem asked. Was Phoebe about to tell her she'd been sent especially for Gem? To save her? To . . . fix her? To make her life less miserable?

"It's like she recognizes you from somewhere," Birdie said, astonished. She almost sounded relieved. "Like she knows you."

"No," Phoebe said, abandoning Gem and giving her a scornful look. "For a moment, I thought maybe you were telling the truth."

EIGHT

Birdie

A lot was happening inside Birdie, and she was trying to let none of it show. She was trying to do what she always did, which was play it off. Even as the sight of Phoebe rattled Birdie to her core. It wasn't just her comic strip, or the painful reality that Gem had stopped reading it. It was so much more than that.

When Birdie was in second grade, she'd broken her arm on the ninja rope line in Gem's backyard. Birdie's lunge off the trapeze was reckless (her mother's word), the break was complicated (the doctor's word), and two weeks after Birdie had the purple cast put on, it still felt like someone had lit her bones on fire (Birdie's words). Her arm wasn't healing. It was getting worse. And when the grown-ups finally figured out why, Birdie had to have surgery to relocate her elbow. Like her elbow was a toddler who'd wandered off at the mall.

Coming out of anesthesia was the first time Birdie saw Phoebe. It was one of those dreams where you're not in the dream, just watching it from outside. She dreamed of a winged creature holding a fishing pole over a golden well. Weird, but then, dreams were weird.

The second time Birdie saw the creature, the scene was the same, only Birdie lingered longer, until the creature fished out a wriggling, golden fish. It wasn't actually a fish. Birdie just called it that because she didn't have a better word for the shimmery, living slip of gold.

"I'll grant you," the winged creature said to the golden glint at the end of her pole.

For weeks after, while Birdie recovered from the surgery, her pain medication causing her to doze off in music class when she should have been banging a xylophone, she would see the creature at the well. And because the creature sometimes talked to herself, Birdie came to know her as Phoebe.

In second grade, Birdie didn't question these dreams. She didn't have to make space for them in a *wonderland* section of her brain so that they could sit next to the *pot-roast-for-dinner reality* section of her brain. She just took it on faith that Phoebe was real, living on a distant star. That the two of them were somehow connected.

She told Gem about Phoebe, of course, and Gem believed her, or said she did. But when they played, they lived out Gem's fantasies, not Birdie's dreams. They searched her yard many times for unicorn hoofprints, but they never made golden fishing poles out of sticks.

Birdie couldn't say precisely when she'd stopped believing in Phoebe. It wasn't like flipping a switch. It was more like, gradually, Birdie's life filled up with other stuff. There was algebra and volleyball and sleepover birthday parties where you had to be the last person awake or else your spare underwear would get frozen. And eventually, there was just less room for Phoebe. It was almost like Birdie forgot about her.

Until the day last year when Birdie needed an idea to submit to the middle school comics contest. And all of a sudden, without Birdie even thinking about it, Phoebe LaCroix had flowed out of the tip of Birdie's pen. The character looked like the creature from Birdie's dreams, but she acted, more or less, like Birdie. Birdie made her the villain, because that seemed like fun, a way to try out her own darkest impulses without any of the consequences.

Birdie won the comics contest, thereby securing *Phoebe LaCroix* a regular spot in the *Wonder Gazette*—and Birdie a spot on the newspaper staff. Birdie loved newspaper. It was her thing. Next year she was going to be co-editor, even though she was only a rising seventh grader.

Now, for some reason, something that looked like Phoebe, and talked like Phoebe, and called itself Phoebe, was *here*—in the woods near Gem's house. Birdie did not feel grateful to encounter the creature in the flesh. She felt scared. Everything about the fairy showing up in Birdie's waking life felt 150 percent wrong.

Which was why it would definitely be better if this whole thing was just a trick someone was playing on Birdie. But who? She squinted at Phoebe, and Phoebe squinted back. Suspicion brewed between them.

"What's wrong with your wings?" Birdie asked.

"Nothing at all." Phoebe spread her dirty wings and bent her knees and kicked herself off the ground. For a moment, she hovered right at Birdie's eye level. "See? They're in perfect order." She beat her wings, but instead of rising, she thumped to the ground.

"Phoebe!" Gem said, falling to her knees. "Are you okay?"

Tiny tears filled Phoebe's eyes as she glared up at Birdie, clutching one webbed foot.

"Your wings are damaged, Phoebe," Van said. "Let me help you. You should rest."

"No indeed! No thank you!" But the fairy's lip quivered

the way Birdie's did when she was bottling up big feelings. "Well, perhaps if there's a glass hut nearby. Something with a view of the stars?"

Over the fairy's head, Van met Birdie's eyes. *Glass hut,* they mouthed.

Just like in Birdie's comic.

Birdie was too weirded out to appreciate Van's interest in her oeuvre. She shrugged it off. "Coincidence," she said.

"My da has a solarium," Van said. "It has a glass ceiling."

"Seriously?" Birdie said.

"I can take her there," Van said. "You two don't have to come—"

"How nosy are your parents?" Gem asked.

"Pretty nosy," Van acknowledged.

"Well, scratch that," Birdie said, then: "My parents don't notice anything." It suddenly occurred to her that if she could talk to Phoebe alone, the two of them could get a few things straight. Like who sent Phoebe. Like how the creature needed to make herself scarce ASAP.

"But you don't have a solarium," Gem said.

"I have a roof," Birdie said. "You can see the stars from it—"

"We are not putting Phoebe on your apartment roof," Gem said.

"Do you have a better idea?" Birdie asked.

"What are the coordinates of your solarium?" Phoebe asked Van, her chin jutting skyward. "I shall take my chances with the Parent Nosies."

It was clear that the creature wanted their help about as much as Birdie wanted to help her, which was not at all. If Birdie had been alone, she could have walked away right now and pretended this whole thing had never happened. But then she looked at Gem. Gem had that look in her eyes like she'd had the day they found the baby bird with the broken wing on the stoop of Birdie's apartment. Birdie remembered how much fun they'd had learning how to nurse a baby bird. They'd fed it baby formula with a mashed-up hard-boiled egg off the tip of a maple leaf. For days, its care consumed them. The day the bird finally took flight, Gem and Birdie could not stop grinning, could not stop hugging.

It made Birdie wonder: If she could just get on board with Phoebe, could she and Gem bond over this broken creature too?

"Evaaaaaaaaaaa?" A woman's shrill voice rang out from beyond the woods.

Van flinched, then cleared their throat and pretended they hadn't heard anything.

The journalist in Birdie took note. "Is that your mom? Is she calling . . . you?"

"She's *not* my mom," Van snapped. "And that's *not* my name."

"Right," Birdie said. She'd hate it too if she identified as *they*, and had adjusted her name, and wardrobe, and probably lots of other things, and her parents pretended none of it was happening, which, let's face it, was exactly what Birdie's parents would do.

"Is your not-mom going to come looking for you?" Gem asked Van.

"I don't think so. She's too lazy, but . . ." Van trailed off.

In that empty space, Birdie understood their situation. Even though it felt like the world had stopped the moment she laid eyes on Phoebe, pretty soon their grown-ups would want them back. They needed to find a place to stash the creature before anyone saw.

"Crabapples," Birdie said.

"Who are they?" Phoebe asked, frightened.

"Trees," Birdie said. "It's not a glass hut, but it's secret. It's safe. From inside, looking up, there's a view of the stars."

"Good," Gem said, and Birdie felt herself exhale.

Then she remembered something. A glitch in her plan. Marley, who never hung out at the crabapples, had been there earlier that day. He said he'd been making a nest for something. Maybe he'd be gone by now. Birdie thought about mentioning it, but the look on Gem's face—so peaceful and determined—told Birdie not to mess with the moment just yet. If Marley was still there, they'd kick him out.

"Where are the crabapples?" Van asked.

"C'mon," Birdie said. "We'll show you."

NINE

Gem

Gem felt a tinge of jealousy as Van scooped Phoebe up. She knew it was childish, but she wanted to be the one to hold the fairy, to smooth Phoebe's hair and tell her it would be okay.

"I am perfectly capable of escorting myself!" Phoebe said, kicking against Van's grip.

"Not outside these woods you aren't," Birdie said. "If one grown-up sees you on the street, we're all screwed."

"Grown-Up?" Phoebe forced a laugh. "I'm not falling for that. I know Grown-Ups are fabrications. The stuff of folklore."

"Here we go again," Van said.

"Sometimes we *wish* grown-ups were fabrications," Gem offered.

"They're mythical monsters. *Mythical*," Phoebe insisted, but her wings had begun to tremble.

"Oh, they're real all right," Birdie said, wagging her fingers menacingly at the fairy. "And this moon is chock full of them. Be afraid!"

"Stop it, Birdie!" Gem said, leading the way over the elm roots, then back across the creek. "Just stay quiet," she told Phoebe. "We'll let you know when it's safe."

In Van's arms, Phoebe scrunched her eyes closed and tensed her tiny muscles, chanting something under her breath that reminded Gem of the way adults at her synagogue said prayers. The fairy was clearly uneasy, but Gem knew if they could just get her to the crabapples, she'd be safe.

Gem was glad they'd settled on that site. She could look out her window tonight and feel that Phoebe was okay. But what did a broken-winged fairy need to make it through the night? What would heal her wings? Not chicken soup and orange juice and a free pass to watch YouTube in bed. What could they serve her that would taste like stardust tea? And what about tomorrow? If Phoebe still couldn't fly in the morning, what would be their plan?

It was getting dark. Shadows stretched across the trees. Gem already knew how hard it would be to leave the fairy, to go inside and eat her mom's roast chicken and act like what was happening here hadn't happened at all.

She winced, remembering what she'd said to her mom earlier. Sometimes words came out of Gem before she knew what she was saying.

She would think about that later. Right now, she could only think about getting Phoebe to the crabapples without being seen. She looked at Birdie, at Van. For better or worse, they were a team now. Phoebe needed them.

Gem led them out of the woods. She felt anxious, in a hurry to make it across the alley. They had to get through the thorny, narrow path between the Barons' and the Groths' yards, then onto the cul-de-sac, and finally, into the crabapples. Their steps quickened. Gem kept looking back to make sure Van still had Phoebe.

"Evening, Gem. Kids," a man's voice called out.

Gem skidded to a halt at the edge of Mr. Groth's front yard. His grass was high and full of crickets.

"Hi, Mr. Groth," she called to the half-deaf old man inching forward on his walker. Why couldn't it have been his wife they'd run into? Mrs. Groth was half-blind.

Gem wanted to make a run for it, before Mr. Groth started asking about school and summer and whether Gem was still dancing. But she knew that would be suspicious, would result in a call to her mom. Their street prided itself on neighborliness.

"How's school?" Mr. Groth called.

"Great!" Gem said, blocking Van and the fairy with her body.

"Almost summer?"

"Yep!"

"Still dancing?"

"Uh-huh," Gem lied. Were they finished yet?

She felt Mr. Groth look past her, to Van, and Gem's heart sank. She knew they didn't deserve to look after a fairy if they couldn't even sneak her past an old man. Gem turned, following her neighbor's eyes. Van's face was white, their body rigid, and their arms were . . . empty?

"Where'd she go?" Gem demanded.

"Huh?" Van said, their tone bewildered, their arms still in the shape of the fairy's form, just holding on to *nothing*.

"She was just there," Gem whispered fiercely, "and now—"

"Everything okay, kids?" Mr. Groth asked.

"Fine!" all three of them shouted, even as Gem rushed to Van. She blinked and—was she seeing things? Because there, in Van's arms, *was* Phoebe. Then . . . no, there she *wasn't*. There she was again, but faded, almost holographic, blinking in and out of visibility. The fairy appeared to be on the fritz, like the TV at Gem's grandma's house. Before Gem could reach out to touch the fairy, Birdie bellowed—

"Hey, Mr. Groth! You got your new issue of *Woodman Life* magazine!"

Gem spun to see Birdie at her neighbor's mailbox, digging out the contents. Now Birdie jogged up the path to deliver the haul to the man.

"Bless you, my girl." He beamed at Birdie, waved the stack of mail in thanks, and turned his walker slowly around to head inside.

Gem, Van, and Birdie waited until his door closed. Then they sprinted for the crabapples.

"Is it gone?" Phoebe asked, voice bobbing as Van ran.

"Stay quiet," Van said. Then, glancing at Gem: "Why'd you freak out? I had her in my arms the whole time."

"I don't know. I didn't see her," Gem admitted as they jogged into the street. "I can't explain it. I thought she was gone." In truth, Phoebe still looked strange to Gem, not quite solid.

"Well, Birdie saved us with the mail," Van said.

"Yeah, thanks Birdie," Gem said. "How'd you know to do that?"

"I can see his house from the crabapples. He always gets his mail this time of day."

If you paid Gem a million dollars, she wouldn't have been able to tell you what time Mr. Groth got his mail. Birdie's attention to detail about stuff that seemed like it would *never* matter to Gem would probably, one day, make

Birdie a really good reporter. Until then, sometimes it just made Birdie seem like she thought she was right about everything. Which, in this case, she was.

"You okay, Gem?" Birdie asked.

"Sure. I think."

As they reached the crabapples, with their hot pink and welcoming arms, Gem noticed that Phoebe looked regular again. Maybe Gem had just had something in her eye? Maybe she needed to eat more carrots? Get more sleep?

At the gap in the crabapples where they always stepped through, Birdie stopped.

"What are you waiting for?" Gem asked.

"We have to do the thing," Birdie said through her teeth.

"Birdie, this is no time for—"

"It's bad luck if we don't do the Crank, and you know it."

Gem sighed. She did know it. She turned to Van and Phoebe, glancing past them to check that no one was watching. "So this place, it's, like, our secret hideout. We inherited it from my neighbor/ex-babysitter when she went to college, and no one's allowed inside but us."

"Oh." Van nodded. They started to turn away. "Should have known."

"We're making an exception," Birdie said, taking Van by the elbow. "But you have to learn the dance."

"Dance?"

"Uh-huh," Birdie said. "You don't have to do it every time, just this first time. Phoebe, you've got to do it too."

"I am an excellent dancer," the fairy proclaimed.

"I am . . . not," Van said.

"It's easy," Birdie said. "Even I can do it."

"Watch and learn," Gem said, and then she and Birdie modeled the Crabapple Crank. First a shoulder shimmy forward, then a shoulder shimmy back, two jumps to the left, a lookout pose, a right knee slap into the Superman. The two girls turned to Van. It was their turn.

Van closed their eyes. Opened them. "You can't laugh. No one can laugh."

"Promise," Gem said.

"Swear," Birdie said.

Van took a deep breath, then placed Phoebe on the ground. "Here goes nothing."

The second time, all four of them did it, and Gem wasn't sure who was funnier to watch—Van or the fairy. Still, she held her laughter in; she had promised Van.

Only by the middle of the Crank, it was Van who started laughing. Nervously at first, but then a real, big, powerful laugh came out of the new kid.

"Changed my mind," Van said through a fit of giggles. "We can laugh."

And so they did, even Phoebe, cracking up hard as

they finished the Crank. And that was when Gem decided to stop thinking of Van as the new kid. Van was just a kid, one who'd found a fairy and was sharing her, one who Gem and Birdie were about to invite into their most sacred space.

Gem was glad Birdie had insisted on the ritual. It felt right when the two of them pointed the way in through the gap in the branches.

"Now," they said together, as Gem's ex-babysitter had once said to them, "you are welcome to the crabapples."

TEN

Van

Van was standing in a place so enchanting it didn't feel real. *The crabapples.* Two large trees whose blooming boughs tangled round each other like a hot-pink force field. There was just space enough at the base of the trunks for the kids to gather, and—most amazing of all—you couldn't see anything outside. Like the rest of the world had been taken away, or else the kids and the fairy had. Looking up, Van found a nice view of the sky, just as Phoebe requested. If there was a good place in this part of Texas for a possible fairy to recover, this was it.

Still, was it weird that Van was here? Did Birdie and Gem want them here? Or did they only want the fairy, and it would have been rude—not to mention impossible—to leave Van out of things? Maybe Phoebe was like a group project at school: you didn't have to be friends with your collaborators to share the same goal of getting a good grade.

Gem had gone to her kitchen to grab supplies, with some special instructions from Van. Birdie was high in the boughs, keeping watch. She seemed on edge, like she still suspected someone of playing a trick on her. Van didn't know what to make of how much Birdie had gotten right about the creature in her comic, but it was clear Birdie didn't want to talk about it. At least not with Van. Van sat next to Phoebe, their back against a trunk.

"We really are in Texas, aren't we?" the fairy said in a breathless voice.

"We really are."

The fairy closed her eyes. "And that monster out there . . ."

"He really is a grown-up," Van said. "He seemed all right, as far as his kind go."

"Why do you allow them in your midst?"

Van laughed. "They're in charge. It's just the way it is."

Phoebe seemed to struggle to accept this. "I *saw* him. He didn't see me, thank the stars, because I put up a glamour to ward off monsters' eyes. But I saw him."

"Does that mean that you believe in grown-ups now?"

Van asked. If she did, wouldn't that be a slippery slope to believing in children?

Phoebe shook her head. "Don't you know how glamours work?"

"Actually," Van said, "not really." Their gran back in Ireland used to talk of glamours, a kind of spell the fairies used depending on whether they wanted to be noticed or blend in. But of course Van didn't know how they *worked*.

"They're general," Phoebe explained, "like wishes themselves. Broad. I threw up a standard glamour against monsters, added in a line about Grown-Ups, which means that Mr. Groth—not to mention your friend Gem—could be any form of evil incarnate."

"What's it got to do with Gem?" Birdie called from her tree bough. Van hadn't realized she was listening. They hoped they hadn't said anything stupid.

"When I had the glamour up," Phoebe said, "Gem couldn't see me either. There's something bad in her. If I were you, I'd beware."

Van and Birdie shared a look. Something *had* happened out there that prevented Gem from seeing Phoebe. Birdie appeared to be chewing on this too. Gem didn't seem like a monster to Van. Maybe a little full of herself, but so were tons of kids. What could Phoebe sense in Gem that they couldn't?

"Phoebe, why don't you believe in children?" Birdie asked.

"Because if it's true, it's too terrible."

"What's too terrible?" Van asked. "What do you mean—"

"Shhh!" Phoebe stiffened at the sound of Gem's footsteps on the other side of the crabapples.

"Look," Van said quickly. "I know you don't believe in us yet, but just"—how to phrase it? Van thought of this weird thing their mam said when she was trying to stretch one of Van's firmly held opinions—"just let the possibility marinate."

"Marinate?" Phoebe and Birdie said at the same time.

"It means to infuse. To slowly soak up—like, a sauce, or in this case, an idea. It's a cooking metaphor. My mam has dozens of them, which is funny because she gets stressed out boiling an egg."

"My mom sucks at cooking too," Birdie said, and Van locked eyes with her again, only this time, it was less awkward. They had something else in common.

That's when Gem appeared back at their side looking very undangerous, setting down a tea tray with four mugs and a kettle. She passed a shrink-wrapped packet to Van.

"Best I could do."

"'Dried imported porcini stems,'" Van read. They'd asked Gem to bring out some mushrooms, but these looked fancy enough that one of Gem's parents would surely miss them soon. And Van didn't even know if their idea would work. It was far-fetched, to say the least.

"Let's give her the tea first," Van said.

Gem set a mug before Phoebe, whose nose twitched to attention. She tried to lift her mug, but it was too big, too heavy, so Van raised it to Phoebe's lips.

"Wait," Gem said, "it's not really—"

But Phoebe was already drinking deeply. She didn't come up for air until the cup was empty and tea ran down her chin.

"Delicious, but impostor," she said sadly.

"Yeah, we didn't have stardust," Gem said. "It's chamomile. But I put a lot of honey in."

"Chamomile?" Phoebe squinted down into the cup.

"It's a flower," Gem said. "I think. Like the petals on your hat?"

The fairy touched the fragile petals making up her red hat. "There are no flowers where I come from. My bonnet is made of the cosmos."

"She didn't know what puppies were either," Van said. "Phoebe, how did you learn English?"

Phoebe looked at them blankly. "What's English?"

"Our language," Van said. "This language. Do you speak all languages?"

"Do you know French?" Gem asked. *"Comment allez-vous?"*

"Pig Latin?" Birdie called from up in the tree. *"Ooh-hay ent-say ooh-yay?"*

"I am speaking in my native tongue," Phoebe said. "I used a glamour so we can understand each other."

"What's a glamour?" Gem asked.

"It's like a magical shield," Van explained.

"She seems to have a few of them up her sleeve," Birdie added.

"Millions," Phoebe corrected. "And if I were to drop this particular glamour, I would sound like this." A noise came out of the fairy then that was so bottomlessly deep and rumbling, it sounded like a thunderstorm inside a black hole. Van curled into a fetal position to withstand it. Birdie fell out of her tree.

"Go back to the glamour," Birdie said, cupping her ears. "I beg you."

Phoebe blinked, nodded once, and with her glamour up again, she said in a quiet voice, "I don't know what to do. I can't get home if my wings don't work. My wings won't heal if I don't grant wishes. And I can't grant wishes now that I know Children don't exist. I'm doomed."

"Are you saying your wings are powered by granting wishes?" Van asked.

"How else would I fly?" the fairy said.

"There's got to be a way we can convince you that kids are real," Gem said. "If you believed again, you could grant wishes, and then your wings would get better, right?"

"In theory, yes," Phoebe said. "In practice, I'm doomed." She began to cry. "I'm very tired. Someone, please, punch me in the face."

"Did she just say what I think she just said?" Birdie asked.

Phoebe tilted her face toward them, closed her eyes. "Knock me out. I'm ready." When no one moved, the fairy opened her eyes. "It's how we get to sleep back home."

"Doesn't it hurt?" Gem said.

"That's the point! We sleep the pain off! Why? What knocks you out on this planet?"

"Podcasts?" Gem said.

"Meditation," Van said.

They looked to Birdie, but she didn't answer. Instead she narrowed her eyes at Phoebe. "I'll punch you in the face."

"Birdie!" Gem said, but the fairy had already positioned herself in front of Birdie, eyes closed, face tilted up.

Birdie studied Phoebe. Looked down at her fist. Back up at Phoebe. She sucked in her breath, reared back, and clocked the fairy square between the eyes.

Phoebe teetered. Her head lolled. Then she collapsed, grinning, into a pile of twigs and leaves that looked a lot like a bed, and just the right size for the fairy.

"I owe you one," Phoebe said, and promptly started snoring.

"I hope you didn't give her a concussion," Gem said. "Now what?"

Van tore open the package of dehydrated mushrooms. It was better that Phoebe was already asleep; otherwise she'd probably never agree to what Van was about to do. They emptied the mushrooms out onto the tea tray, splashed some of the hot liquid on top. The shriveled-up mushrooms swelled and unfurled, reminding Van of a zombie movie they'd recently turned off.

"What are you doing?" Gem asked.

There wasn't judgment in her voice, only curiosity, so Van decided to explain.

"In my old neighborhood, my friends and I used to find mushrooms growing wild, springing up in shapes like rings. My gran always said that if a child sleeps inside a circle of mushrooms, they gain the second sight." Van met the eyes of the others. "The sight reveals the Fair Folk."

"Fair Folk?" Gem said.

"Leprechauns. Trolls. All manner of fairy creatures."

"So you believe in her," Birdie said.

"I don't know what I believe, okay?" Van said. "But right now, that's not the point. I only know she doesn't believe in *us*. She can't see us properly. And she needs to, or else . . ." Van gestured at Phoebe's pathetic-looking wings. "So let's make her a fairy ring to sleep in, and—"

"Maybe it will have the reverse effect," Gem filled in.

"Right." Van nodded. "Maybe tomorrow, she'll be able to see."

Birdie picked up a mushroom, wrinkling her nose. "This is so not going to work."

"Still," Gem said, "it's worth a shot."

"Gem?" a voice called from beyond the crabapples. "Dinnertime!"

"My mom," Gem whispered, then: "Five more minutes!"

"Come on," Van whispered, wedging the floppy, wet mushrooms into the dirt. Gem and Birdie did the same, and soon enough, they'd made a ring around the fairy. It didn't look like the real ones back home, but it would have to do.

"You'll be safe here," Van whispered. They didn't know if it was true, but then, it *had* to be true. Like when Van watched #itgetsbetter videos on YouTube. "We'll come back in the morning."

As soon as they said this, they looked at the others, embarrassed. They'd just assumed future plans with Birdie and Gem. Why had they done that? Now the girls would think—

But the girls were nodding, like Van had put into words what they were already about to say. Like, of course all three of them would come back tomorrow.

And that might have been the most miraculous part of Van's day.

ELEVEN

Birdie

That night, while her mom jabbed buttons on the microwave, Birdie pet the cat and thought about wishes. Had she made a wish four years ago in the era of her broken arm? Had she *summoned* Phoebe? Who could remember that far back? But even if second-grade Birdie had wished for something, it hadn't come true. Otherwise, wouldn't Birdie's life be better?

Which meant Phoebe wasn't who she claimed to be.

"Set the table, Birdie," her mother said, pulling a single-serve frozen lasagna out of the microwave. Birdie's dad wouldn't be home, again.

Setting the table meant moving the cat, grabbing a

couple of paper plates, the water pitcher, the hot sauce, which Birdie's mom put on everything, and the green canister of parmesan, which Birdie put on everything.

When Birdie's mom sat down, she sighed like the effort of nuking those noodles had taken everything out of her. She ran a knife down the middle of the container, halving it.

Birdie wanted to eat fast and go to her room. She wanted to close the door and think.

"Don't shovel," her mom said.

Birdie slowed down as much as she could, tried to match her mother's methodical forkfuls. She wondered if she'd ever told her mom about Phoebe. Didn't Birdie used to tell her mother everything that passed through her mind? Didn't Phoebe pass through Birdie's mind a lot four years ago? It was hard to remember a time when it had been easy to talk to her mom. It seemed to Birdie that her mother had looked this tired, and her dad had been stuck at the office this late, and they'd been eating this frozen lasagna this tensely, every night for eleven years.

"Are you calling me from the SpaghettiOs section?" Gem said by way of answering the phone. She thought it was hilarious that Birdie called her from the walk-in pantry—the most private place her phone cord stretched—and also that Birdie's pantry was full of crap that Gem's mom would never let her eat but Gem thought was delicious.

"More of a ramen section at the moment," Birdie said,

wedging herself in her usual spot between a case of paper towels and a jumbo bag of cat litter.

"I'm glad you called," Gem said.

The simple words made Birdie feel better. "You are?"

"Wasn't that amazing today? I can't stop thinking about her."

"Me neither." *But not in a good way.* Birdie knew she was being too negative. Gem thought Phoebe's arrival was amazing. Gem wanted to share that amazement with Birdie. Like the old days. Which was what Birdie wanted more than anything. Birdie had to find a way to enjoy this new development, to push aside what Phoebe's arrival really felt like, which was . . .

Well, Birdie hadn't figured that out exactly yet. It was complicated.

"I've been thinking," Gem said. "If the mushroom ring second-sight thing doesn't work . . . I think we should take Phoebe to school."

"What?" Birdie gasped, feeling like she'd just swallowed an entire sack of flour. Her mouth went dry. Her stomach sank.

"You know Ms. Sae Tang's always telling us *Show don't tell* in Writers' Workshop. *Telling* Phoebe about children isn't enough. We need to take her out in the world and *show* her."

"Yeah, but . . ." Birdie struggled to find the right tone

here. She knew where Gem was coming from—Birdie was a writer, strong at both summary (the telling) and scene (the showing). The journalist in her knew to balance primary sources with the research that gave a story context. But when you showed in a story, there was no risk. When you showed a fairy in real life, a million things could go wrong. "What if someone sees her?"

"We'll keep her in my backpack. She'll fit perfectly. I'll pad it with bubble wrap. We'll be careful. Think about it: Where else can she see so many kids? Where better to prove to her we're real?"

Birdie didn't have an answer. All Birdie had was five-alarm panic.

"So, you're in?" Gem said. "Let's call Van and tell her."

"Tell *them*."

"Right. Sorry. I can three-way them."

"Wait. Gem—"

"What?" Gem said.

Birdie took a deep breath. "Do you remember in second grade, I used to have these dreams about a creature who went fishing in a well?"

"I don't think so." Gem laughed. "Your dreams are crazy."

"I told you about it. It was when I broke my arm—"

"Birdie, why are you changing the subject?"

Birdie swallowed. How could she explain that she

wasn't changing the subject? That she and Phoebe sort of . . . went way back?

No, Birdie wasn't ready.

"I remember all *your* old stuff," she found herself saying. "Your make-believe unicorn, Shiloh? I even remember she had a purple mane and silver hooves."

She couldn't help feeling let down that Gem didn't remember. Like her rich inner life didn't matter to Gem. Was forgettable to Gem.

"And the award for best memory goes to . . . Birdie Borovsky," Gem joked.

"I have so many people to thank." Birdie played along at making an acceptance speech.

The thing was, she remembered her whole friendship with Gem because it mattered to her. What did it say that Gem *didn't* remember? Birdie hated when a thought led her to a dark dead end like this.

"You know what else I remember?" Birdie decided to say. "After I broke my arm, you made that pretend cast for your arm. You said you were going to keep it on the whole time I had to wear mine. That was really nice. I probably didn't even thank you then."

"You'd have done the same for me," Gem said. "Can I call Van now?"

Would Birdie have done the same thing, though? Because just then Birdie remembered something else, which was how she'd really felt when Gem showed her the pretend cast. She had felt *bad*. Like she was holding Gem back from having fun. Like, if it weren't for Birdie's dumb broken arm, Gem would be swimming and playing soccer. It had made Birdie feel so bad she got queasy and actually threw up.

And suddenly Birdie knew what was bugging her about the Phoebe situation:

It felt like someone was dragging Birdie backward in time, in maturity, all the way to second grade. Birdie couldn't afford the missed ground. She was behind Gem enough as it was.

Why couldn't Phoebe have fallen to earth four years ago, when Birdie believed in her? Not now, when the fairy felt like the world's most embarrassing secret.

Gem wanted to take Phoebe out of the crabapples. It spelled bad news for Birdie. Because embarrassing secrets had ways of getting out.

What next? Would the pastor at church work it into a sermon that Birdie had wet the bed one random night last summer? Would the Wonder Middle Twitter account tweet out that until fourth grade she'd worn Dora the Explorer underpants?

By now, there had been a long silence on the phone. Birdie should absolutely fill it with a laundry list of reasons why taking Phoebe out and about was a terrible idea.

But she didn't, because that would be *choosing* to drive yet another wedge in her friendship with Gem. No, she wouldn't do that. She would choose Gem. Always.

"Okay," she breathed.

"Great," Gem said. "I'm dialing."

Birdie heard the click of her friend switching over to her other line. She closed her eyes and tried to reset all her feelings. Gem came back with Van.

"Hey, Birdie," Van said.

"Are you in or are you out?" Birdie asked.

"I'm in," Van said. "I'm definitely in."

TWELVE

Gem

When they met at the crabapples the next morning before school, the fairy was chewing on Gem's dad's twenty-dollar mushrooms.

"I don't think it worked," Van admitted.

"Phoebe," Gem said, "how would you feel about coming to school with us today?"

"What is this 'school'?" Phoebe asked.

"Oh, just this super-boring place where we're made to spend fifty percent of our waking hours," Birdie said.

"School is a place for learning," Gem cut in. "In your case, about children. Being real." She looked at the others. "We'll split up the class periods. I'll keep Phoebe first and second. Van, you can have her third and fourth. Birdie, take fifth and sixth?"

"Not me," Birdie said. "I lose things." She popped out the cherry-red expander from her bottom teeth with her tongue and lisped: "This is my third one of these."

Gem remembered how mad Birdie's mom had been when Birdie left her first expander on the armrest of her seat at the movie theater. She'd turned the car around after picking them up, then made them crawl around on the floor looking. They had to go through the movie theater trash, which had been so disgusting it was almost funny, and Birdie and Gem had gotten into an epic popcorn-throwing fight. But they still didn't find the expander, and Birdie had cried on the way home while her mom yelled about the cost of the replacement. And then Birdie lost the replacement. Gem was glad she hadn't been around Birdie's mom that day.

"You two take her," Birdie said. "Van and I have science together, so I'll see her in fifth."

"That works," Gem said, smiling. "It means I can have her for third period, and we're watching the *Babies* documentary in social studies. That should be convincing."

From the base of the tree, Phoebe cleared her throat. "Don't I get a say in this?"

Van knelt down to her. "What do you say?"

"I say, I am not getting in there!" She pointed at the

sequined backpack, which Gem had spent two hours the night before padding with bubble wrap and securing with tape and generally getting just right for taking a fairy to school.

Instead of a zipper, her backpack had a drawstring top, then a flap that covered the drawstring and closed with a snap. Phoebe could peer out through the gap. Gem had put her favorite body butter—the fairy's webbed feet could use a little TLC—and a couple of stuffed animals inside, plus a small pad of paper and one of her dad's golf pencils in case Phoebe wanted to take notes. She'd packed snacks.

"Well, we tried," Birdie said with a shrug. "But if Phoebe doesn't consent..."

"We can't give up that easy," Gem said, annoyed. The bell would ring in twenty minutes, and they needed to get the fairy into the bag. If they didn't, and they left for school without Phoebe, then today would be hell, just like yesterday.

But with Phoebe in her bag, Gem would have a purpose. She wouldn't be the butt of some perverted bully's joke; she'd be a girl with magic at her back.

Magic that Felix Howard couldn't touch.

But what was Gem supposed to do—beg?

Van crouched down to Phoebe and placed cupped hands on the dirt. When Phoebe stepped aboard, Van lifted the fairy to eye level.

"I was scared on my first day of school. I didn't know a soul. And honestly, some parts were awful. But you have us. And we'll take care of you. You do *want* to believe in children, don't you?"

Phoebe didn't answer, but the way she averted her eyes gave Gem the sense that something bad had happened to the fairy, that she wasn't being stubborn for the fun of it, that she was truly scared to risk believing.

"I made you tea," Van said, taking a thermos from their backpack. Why hadn't Gem thought of that? "Eight parts honey."

Phoebe reached for the thermos, but Van nodded gently toward Gem's backpack. A bargain. Finally the fairy sighed and tucked her tattered wings behind her. She climbed inside.

Gem thrilled at Phoebe's weight when she shouldered the straps. The fairy was about as heavy as one of the sacks of oranges that Gem's mom bought at Sam's Club. Van slipped in the thermos, tightened the drawstring, and snapped the flap. A moment later, the three of them heard slurping. Gem smiled.

"Come on," she said, and led the way to school.

Wonder Middle School was half a mile away from Gem's front door, and this was the first year she was allowed to walk by herself or with friends. Gem's brother, Marley, who went to Wonder Elementary on the same campus, still had to be walked down by one of their parents. But luckily, his school started half an hour earlier, so Marley and her dad were long gone.

When they reached the front gates, Gem remembered how yesterday, when the bell rang, she'd told herself she didn't have to come back here for sixteen entire hours. It had helped.

Today felt different. Today felt lighter. It didn't mean Gem hated Felix Howard any less, or that she was not self-conscious about her T-shirt clinging to her chest. It was just . . . today there was more to life than there'd been yesterday. And the new stuff, Gem believed, was good stuff. She liked walking into school with Gem and Van on either side of her. She liked making a plan to meet at lunch, not at her regular table with Birdie, but along the wall outside.

It was cooler—socially and air-conditioning-wise—to sit in the cafeteria. Which made outside along the wall perfect for their meeting today. They could be alone.

Gem felt Phoebe wriggling. She must have finished her tea.

"We're here," Gem told her, peering through the gap.

"Wh-what's all that out there?" the fairy whispered, sounding suddenly timid.

"That is childhood," Gem explained. "If Birdie, Van,

and I didn't convince you, maybe five hundred and twenty-three other kids will."

She tried to see the mayhem of the schoolyard through the fairy's eyes. The screaming, running packs of kids. The masses of them streaming out of buses. The half-asleep stragglers circling back to parents' cars to grab forgotten backpacks. Did Phoebe feel as overwhelmed as Gem had felt her first day of middle school? Did she think the students looked as huge and intimidating as Gem had?

"Fairy in distressssss!" came Phoebe's voice from the backpack as she tried to launch herself out of the sequined top flap.

The fairy was out almost as far as her wings when Birdie caught her. She tamped Phoebe roughly back inside Gem's bag. She seized the little belay clip on the interior lining that Gem sometimes used to attach her water bottle and clipped it to a belt loop at the back of Phoebe's dress.

"Stop that! HELP!" Phoebe writhed and fought Birdie closing the flap. Gem's eyes darted around the schoolyard to check who else had seen. Strangely, no one had.

"Good job," Gem breathed. "Quick thinking. That was almost really bad."

Birdie played it off, but Gem noticed her hands were trembling.

"Phoebe," Van said, their voice low near the backpack flap. "You *can't* do that again."

"But someone out there might tell me the truth," Phoebe said.

"You're here to observe, not to *be* observed," Gem said. "It would be dangerous if anyone else saw you."

"Wise words from the creatures who have me enslaved in a torture chamber," Phoebe hissed from inside. "Wait, are there Grown-Ups here?"

"Dozens," Birdie said. "So stay in the bag."

"How do I recognize one?" Phoebe asked. Only her eyes now peered out from the flap.

"Taller, older, meaner," Birdie said, gesturing at Miss Tanya, the music teacher, currently cursing the coffee she'd just spilled down her shirt.

"So, that's one there?" Phoebe asked.

Hoisting the bag high on one shoulder, Gem followed the fairy's gaze to Salvador Martin, an eighth grader who was never not dribbling a basketball. He was huge. At lunch he and his friends shot milk out their noses.

"Looks like a grown-up," Gem said, and kept walking, "but very much a child."

"It's called a growth spurt," Birdie said.

"And that one?" The fairy poked a finger out the flap in the direction of Kaitlin Koch, who towered over a circle of girls near the flagpole. Gem had been friends with Kaitlin for fifteen minutes at the start of the year. They had a K-pop crush in common, but that was it.

"Child," Gem said. "She's wearing platforms. It's a shoe. So yeah, there are exceptions. Once we get into class, it'll be easier to tell the difference. The kids all sit in desks."

"Where will I sit?" Phoebe asked, jumping up and down inside Gem's backpack. "I want a desk. What's a desk?"

Gem looked at Birdie, at Van. How many times did they have to go over this?

"You'll be staying put. Remember?" Gem said. "In the backpack, where it's safe."

"But it's dark in here!" Phoebe whined.

Heads turned in their direction at the sound of Phoebe's increasingly loud voice. Gem wondered whether the fairy's glamour extended to other kids' ears. Before Gem could think up a distraction, a distraction found them—a flash of black grew in her peripheral vision. She ducked out of the way, narrowly avoiding Felix Howard, who rolled through campus on his skateboard, which was against school rules.

"Watch it, Cantaloupes," he shouted over his shoulder.

"Shut up, Butt-Ass!" Birdie shouted back.

Butt-Ass? Where had Birdie found that one?

Gem groaned as Felix wheeled back around, coming to a stop right in front of them. Her stomach squeezed like a sponge, and her cheeks felt a thousand degrees.

"What'd you call me?" Felix said, not sure which one of them to interrogate.

"Birdie," Gem muttered through gritted teeth, willing her best friend not to blow it. They had a *fairy* in a *backpack* at *school*.

Somehow Birdie managed to hold her tongue, just glared at him until he got bored.

"That's what I thought," Felix said, unleashing one of his disgusting burps. He circled them on his skateboard again—and just before he skated away, yanked the strap of Gem's backpack so hard she heard a rip. *No*. As Gem fell backward, her mind filled with prayers that she wouldn't crush the fairy. But before she landed anywhere, Van caught her.

"You okay?" Van asked.

"Phoebe," Gem whispered. The three of them huddled around the backpack, trying not to look like they were huddled around the backpack. Felix had ripped the left strap off, but the rest was still intact.

"I'm fine," Phoebe said from within. "No thanks to that butt-ass." Then the fairy laughed.

Gem laughed. Van laughed. All three of them looked to Birdie.

"It was the first thing that popped into my head!" Birdie said defensively, but finally she laughed too. As the bell rang, Birdie lifted the flap of the backpack. "Don't be a butt-ass, and stay in the bag where it's safe. Low-profile is your middle name."

✳ ✳ ✳

But Phoebe didn't want to be low-profile. Phoebe wanted to make Gem's life impossible. During roll in first period, when Mr. Omar called Ravi Singh's name, instead of saying "Here," he stood up and loudly announced to the class:

"I wish my baby sister had never been born!"

As Ravi clapped a hand over his mouth and sank back down, looking humiliated, Gem tilted her head to gape at Phoebe.

What the heck? Gem mouthed. This was clearly the fairy's doing.

The fairy raised one eyebrow, as if daring Gem to stop her.

"I'll mark you as present, Ravi," Mr. Omar said before straightening his shoulders and adding, in a voice quite unlike the one he taught in: "I wish I had told Anita that I loved her—" He broke off with an embarrassed cough, thumping a fist against his chest.

Gem could risk no further catastrophe. She shouldered her backpack and hurtled toward the door, grabbing the bathroom pass and belting out the fail-safe excuse she'd always been too mortified to use. "Cramps!"

Locking the door of the farthest stall, Gem hung her backpack on the hook inside the door. She waited until two seventh-grade girls finished washing their hands, then jerked open the drawstring.

"What are you doing?" she demanded.

"Learning," Phoebe said. She looked a little peaked. "I've never dropped such unusual glamours. That was exhausting—but exhilarating."

"You dropped my teacher's glamour?" Gem said, cringing. She so did not need to know the confidential details of Mr. Omar's love life. "What does that mean?"

"I dropped the glamours protecting a couple of the wishes in that room," Phoebe corrected. "Wishes are private things. Most creatures don't know that. Most creatures think they themselves are the ones embarrassed of their true wishes. In fact, it's the wishes who are shy. Wishes only like to come out when they trust that they are absolutely safe."

"And you make wishes feel safe when you grant them?" Gem asked, liking the sound of that.

"Of course." Phoebe pressed a hand to her heart. "I treat each one with the tenderest love and mercy."

Gem was touched by Phoebe's sincerity. Then confused. "Wait, you were granting wishes back there? Mr. Omar? Ravi Singh?" She couldn't deny the prospect was exciting. "Wouldn't that help your wings? Does it mean that you believe—"

"No." Phoebe snorted. "I was only examining those wishes, holding them up to the light. Granting is another thing entirely. A project far richer than *you* would understand. No, I can't grant impostor wishes. It would do nothing for me, or the universe."

"Then why—"

"I just wanted you to let me out of the bag."

Gem groaned. "You almost got us both in so much trouble. All I'm trying to do is show you—"

"Well, you can stop. It must be exhausting for you. This performance is elaborate—and transparent!"

How great would it be if Gem's life *was* a performance, and it could end, the curtain drop? She could take a bow to wild applause. She could leave the stage and step out a back door into a different, less embarrassing existence.

"Why don't you just *try* granting one of our wishes? If it comes true, wouldn't that be proof we're kids?"

"I told you. I can't grant *unless* I believe."

"But why not try?" Gem said, even though Phoebe's logic sounded reasonable. Dance was like that too—you had to think you could nail a triple pirouette to be able to nail a triple pirouette.

"Already did," Phoebe said. "Yesterday. With the one called Van. My granting days are over. And you can tell that to the priestess."

Gem cracked her knuckles, thinking. Phoebe was so magical, and so . . . frustrating. If she would only look around, she would see this place was crawling with children. She'd *believe* again, and then they could move on to the wish granting. Selfishly, Gem wanted to get to that part.

Through the crack in the stall, her eyes fell on the feminine-products machine attached to the bathroom wall, and a thought struck her that really did make her stomach cramp.

"I need to tell you something," Gem confessed. "I'm not entirely a child."

Phoebe's eyebrows shot up. "Go on."

"Do you know what a period is?" Gem asked, feeling herself turn pink. "Never mind. Just, a few months ago, this thing happened to me. This super-embarrassing thing. My mom called it a 'rite of passage' and she slapped me, which is customary in the Jewish religion. I know it sounds weird."

Phoebe looked lost. Gem closed her eyes.

"But I'm sort of a woman now."

"You claim to have changed from a Child into a Grown-Up?" Phoebe asked.

"In all the other ways, I'm still a child. I can't drive or vote or eat what I feel like eating for dinner, but . . ." Gem sighed. "I might not be the best guide for you."

"On the street yesterday," Phoebe said slowly, "you couldn't see me, could you?"

Gem shook her head, eyes on her shoes. So many things about growing up sucked. Now here was another to add to the list. She was literally losing sight of the only real magic she'd ever known.

"Not that I believe you," Phoebe said, "but if I did, that would explain what happened with my glamour."

"I want you to believe," Gem said. "If you need a real child to help guide you, you should be with Birdie."

"She'll *lose* me. You heard her."

"She won't," Gem said. "She sells herself short. But when it matters, Birdie always comes through."

Phoebe's lip quivered. Gem felt her heart fold up. She wondered how it felt to be a fairy in a crisis, far from your star. Gem was in a crisis too—the crisis of sixth grade, but at least she had her family. At least she had Birdie.

"I'll never get home," Phoebe wailed.

Thirteen

Van

At lunch that day, Van didn't go to the orchestra room, where they and the other orchestra aids had permission to eat. They went to the wall outside.

It was hot, no shade, and brutally humid. But as soon as Van saw Birdie and Gem, the backpack glittering behind her, they stopped noticing the weather.

They smiled. They couldn't help it. They felt—to use one of their mam's favorite cooking metaphors—like a stick of butter taken out of the fridge: they were beginning to soften. Mam always said softening couldn't be rushed. You didn't put butter in the microwave when you were making shortbread. It just had to sit there, on the counter, until it came to room temperature. Until it was ready to mix with other ingredients. Like Birdie and Gem. Maybe Van was ready now.

"How'd it go?" they asked as Gem set her backpack between them. Trying not to be too obvious—there were kids playing handball at the far end of the wall—Van peeked inside. The fairy looked pent up and ticked off. Kind of like Van's cat, Roscoe, looked when they took him to the vet to get his nails clipped.

"Let's just say we spent a lot of time hiding out in a bathroom stall," Gem said.

For a moment, Gem looked like she was going to say something else about her time with Phoebe. Instead she nudged the backpack in Van's direction. "Hope you have better luck this afternoon."

Gem took out her lunch, a bento box full of cut-up fruits and veg and a turkey sandwich that looked really nice. On days when Van was with their da, they got three dollars and whatever the cafeteria was serving. Today was pizza, from which Birdie was picking off the pepperonis without asking. Birdie's lunch, a Lunchable, she slipped into the fairy backpack.

"Eating keeps her occupied," Birdie said when Gem gave her a look.

Van looked inside Gem's bag and watched the fairy take a nibble.

"Needs honey," she pronounced.

"I was thinking this morning," Van said, taking out their notebook and opening it to a dog-eared page. "About stuff that makes kids kids. I made some notes. Yesterday Phoebe told me she was raised to believe that children are all-knowing. That we only desire what we truly need. And that grown-ups are supposed to be subservient to us."

Birdie whistled. "And they say *our* history books are flawed."

"How did the truth get so warped?" Gem asked.

"Clearly because you're not the real deal," Phoebe called from inside the bag.

"Well," Van said, "there are just other things that make us real." They held their book out.

"These are your notes?" Birdie asked.

Van nodded. Their "notes" had taken the form of a comic strip.

"This is *good*," Birdie said. "You're really good, Van."

Van's heart lifted. How long had they wanted to talk comics with Birdie B? Only every day, all year long.

Leaning against the lip of the backpack, noisily eating a slice of cheese, Phoebe pointed at the drawing of Van blowing out their birthday candles. "What's that?"

"It's a birthday cake," Gem said. "Kids wish on them each year. I bet it's how a lot of wishes reach you."

"Is it a good thing or a bad thing, the life of a Child?" the fairy asked, studying the pages.

"Both," Van, Gem, and Birdie all said together.

"Can I?" Birdie asked, taking out a pencil and pointing at one of the blank panels at the bottom of Van's page. Van had hoped Birdie might collaborate with them.

They slid the notebook closer, held their breath, then watched as Birdie sketched a kid with a broken arm in a cast. The kid was leaning against a windowsill, looking up at a night sky. Birdie added a caption: *Starlight, star-bright . . .*

"Listen, Phoebe," Birdie said. "On a basic level, being a kid is fun. Way more fun than being a grown-up. At the same time, we are not in control. Grown-ups are. Which can suck. So, a lot of times, kids feel trapped." Birdie tapped her pencil against her drawing of the kid. "That's why we wish so much."

Phoebe studied Birdie's drawing. "Why don't Grown-Ups wish?"

"Because—" Birdie said.

"—they have everything they need," Gem said.

"My parents don't." Birdie sounded offended.

"I didn't mean—" Gem said.

"I think maybe grown-ups don't wish," Van said—they were thinking of their chronically overbooked da and his sarcastic girlfriend; they were thinking of their tired mam—"because they don't think it'll change anything."

"Yeah." Birdie nodded. "That's the difference."

Van thought of their last birthday, back in February, at the steakhouse where their parents had actually sat at the same table. They remembered the blank spot in their mind as they blew out the candles. They hadn't even made a wish. Because all they wanted was to move back to Ireland, and that wasn't going to happen, and they couldn't think of anything else they wanted that might possibly come true.

Did that make them a terrible guide for Phoebe? Like, the anti-child? They swallowed an unchewed bite of pizza. It hurt going down their throat.

Birdie was sketching something else in the last panel on the page. The kid with the broken arm had a lasso they were throwing into the sky, toward—

"What's that?" Van asked as the bell rang.

"Nothing," Birdie said, snapping the book closed. "It's not finished."

"Keep it," Van said. "You can give it to me after school."

Birdie nodded, took the notebook just as Gem held out her glittery backpack to Van. Van had thought they'd transfer Phoebe out of the glitter and into Van's black bag. Now they realized there was no safe way of doing that without risking eyes on Phoebe.

So Van was going to carry this pink-and-purple sequined thing around the rest of the afternoon. Was

Gem trying to torture them? No, Van assured themself. There had been a time when this would have felt insulting, when it would have made them want to scream. Today it felt like the only choice to make. So they just made it. They picked up the bag by its remaining strap.

When Gem reached for Van's bag, Van said, "Wait. My flute. I have orchestra next."

"Hope you brought your earplugs, Phoebe," Birdie teased as Van retrieved their flute case from their backpack.

One of the first things Van had learned about Wonder Middle School was that the orchestra was only considered good as the punchline of a joke.

"No offense, Van," Birdie said. "I'm sure you're great."

Van didn't take offense. *Great* was one word for what they were. *Prodigy* was another. They'd been playing the flute since they were five years old and Caro's da showed *embouchure* to them, demonstrating on a soda bottle beneath the dartboard in his pub. Three times, Van had played in the youth orchestra at the National Concert Hall in Dublin. At Wonder, they were first chair, and the second-chair flautist was nice but could hardly read music. There was no philharmonic in this part of Texas, but Van's mom was saving up to take them to Dallas the second weekend of summer break. They were going to see a performance of *Peter Pan* with a live orchestra at the Myerson

Symphony Center. They were going to stay overnight in a hotel and order room service for breakfast the next day. Van couldn't wait.

Birdie was joking about the earplugs, but Van was suddenly glad the fairy had none. Part of being a kid was being bad at things at first, then practicing them until you got good. Van could have drawn that into one of their comic strip panels, but now, in orchestra, Phoebe would see and hear it for herself.

"Meet here after the bell?" Gem said, seeming anxious about letting Van take Phoebe.

"I'll be here," Birdie said.

"Me too." It was the first time all year Van had a plan to meet anyone after school.

Fourteen

Birdie

"Was your afternoon as bad as my morning?" Gem asked Van after school.

"Actually," Van said, "orchestra mellowed her out. Look." They lifted the flap, where inside, the fairy was tranquil, humming.

"Aww," Gem said as they started walking home. "Birdie, look."

"Uh-huh," Birdie said, distracted. She was stuck between a rock and hard place. On one hand, if she showed Phoebe her sketch of the tether between the broken-arm kid and the fairy at the Wishwell, completed in Van's notebook during sixth period, it might jog the fairy's memory—that the two of them were connected, fairy and child, going back years. Proof that both sides were real. On the other hand, it would seal Birdie's fate as the baby of the group. As the little kid who made wishes, who not only believed in this stuff, but who was the reason the fairy was here.

Birdie couldn't figure out whether owning up to her history with Phoebe would do more to sever or save her friendship with Gem. Gem seemed into the fairy today, but at any moment, she might decide that it was immature, and then Birdie would be stuck forever on the wrong side of the line. Even if the fairy did come around to believing they were children, who knew if it would fix her wings? Gem was what Birdie cared about. Gem was the core of her decision. Walking to the crabapples, the notebook burned in her backpack. She didn't know what to do.

"I'm starving," Phoebe said. "What's for lunch?"

The fairy had already plowed through Birdie's Lunchable, Gem's berries, and half of Van's pizza less than two hours ago. As soon as she'd swallowed each item, she'd complained—nothing was sweet enough, and nothing put a dent in her appetite.

"We'll go by my house for snacks," Gem said as they turned onto her cul-de-sac. "Nobody's home."

Birdie, for once, wasn't hungry. She wanted to get to the crabapples. The crabapples centered her. Like base in tag, they were safe. She did some of her best thinking there.

She believed that once they were within the boughs again, she'd know what to do about her drawing and the truth.

But the fairy was hungry, so the fairy would eat.

Gem put her key in the lock and turned. They stepped inside and kicked off their shoes.

"Your parents aren't here?" Van said.

"Not till five thirty."

"And Marley?" Birdie asked.

"Who's Marley?" Van asked.

"My brother. He has Odyssey of the Mind after school on Wednesdays. It's kind of like brain Olympics for gifted kids. And he's not home till after four."

Just the same, Van left Phoebe in the backpack as they followed Gem to the kitchen.

"What are you in the mood for?" Van asked.

"Something I've never tried before!" Phoebe announced. "Something sweet!"

"Wrong house for that," Birdie said, opening Gem's pantry. There were three different bottles of soy sauce. Bags of nuts in bulk. The kind of oatmeal that took half an hour to cook. "Welcome to Health Nut Land."

She found a jar of peanut butter and a glass canister of pretzels.

"Classic childhood combo," Gem said. "You'll love peanut butter, Phoebe. All kids do."

"Except the ones with life-threatening allergies," a disembodied voice called from the other side of the kitchen.

Birdie's, Gem's, and Van's eyes shot across the room to where none of them had noticed Gem's younger brother curled up with the family Great Dane. He was absolutely covered in dog hair.

"Just saying," Marley said, sitting up. "If a sixth grader's never had peanut butter, there's probably a reason." He gestured at Van, the kid he didn't know, the kid he must have assumed had never had peanut butter.

Birdie's heart began to pound. They needed to get Phoebe out of here fast.

"You're supposed to be at OM." Gem's voice was sharp as a blade.

Marley stood up, and when he did, Birdie glimpsed the other side of his face, heretofore hidden in the belly of the giant dog. He had a fat lip and a black eye.

"What happened to you?" Birdie asked, wincing. It looked awful. He should put some ice on the whole situation.

"Got in a fight," Marley mumbled.

"You did not," Gem said, marching toward him, hands on her hips.

"You think I'm lying?"

"Who would *you* get in a fight with?"

"Felix Howard."

Gem opened her mouth, but it was like the words evaporated before they reached her lips.

"Seriously?" Birdie asked, stepping forward to get a better look at that eye. It was bad. And Felix Howard *was* known to terrorize not just the middle school yard but also the elementary school yard on his skateboard after school. But how . . . *why* would Marley have crossed hideous Felix Howard?

"Because of me?" Gem whispered. "Because of yester-day?"

Marley looked away, embarrassed. Gem looked away too. Birdie looked back and forth between them, surprised and confused. She'd spent years of her life with these siblings and had never seen them act anywhere near as awkward as they were right now. Impatient, yes. Annoyed and greedy, violent and generous, bossy, and mind-meldingly in sync. But not *this*, where they couldn't even look each other in the eye.

"Don't you ever think I might be tired of disappearing in a sea full of nerds!" Marley shouted out of nowhere.

"You're such an idiot, Marley," Gem said. "Do you know what I'd give to disappear in a sea of nerds?"

"I wish you would disappear—" Marley started to say before Birdie stepped between them. She pressed the peanut butter into Gem's hands, reminding her best friend of their purpose. It was not to get waylaid by Marley, black eye or not.

"We're leaving," Birdie said. "Marley, put some ice on your bad self." She turned to him. He looked furious, maybe at Felix, maybe at Gem, maybe at the whole hard world. All of which Birdie got.

"And, you know," she added, "props on not dying in your first fight ever, with the meanest kid in town. That's pretty cool." She smiled at Marley, because Gem certainly wasn't going to notice that Marley's fight was an achievement. Ditto his parents; they wouldn't be giving out any awards. Birdie could do this small thing for Marley on her way out the door. "Did you mess him up at all?"

One side of Marley's mouth rose in a smile. "I sort of got a punch in."

"There you go."

Birdie turned to the others, feeling good that she had paved their way to a smooth exit from the kitchen. It could have been bad, but Birdie stepped in, and now it was fine.

And that was when she noticed Van struggling with the backpack. Struggling, more precisely, to keep Phoebe *inside* the backpack.

"Let me out!" the fairy shouted. "LET ME OOOO-OUT!"

Then Phoebe burst through the top flap of the backpack, sailed across the kitchen like a cannonball with wings, and landed—*thump!*—in Marley's arms.

"It's *you*," the fairy cried, holding tight to Gem's little brother as if her whole, precarious life depended on it. "Forgive me!"

FIFTEEN

Marley

"If you must smite me," the creature whispered, holding tight to Marley's neck, "I'll take it bravely."

And just when Marley thought today couldn't get any weirder. Holding this creature wasn't like anything he'd ever done before. It felt like putting his arms around the space between the high dive and the surface of the pool. Marley was scared, and he wanted more, and he couldn't remember how he'd gotten here.

Context clues: He was in his kitchen. His sister, and Birdie, and another kid, were staring at him. The thing in his arms had wings. It seemed to think it knew him. The rest remained a mystery. Usually mysteries excited

Marley. But this one was next-level strange.

He looked to Gem, who was only 501 days older than him, but who acted like someone had hired her to be the boss of Marley's life. When they were young, they used to get mistaken for twins all the time. Not so much because they looked alike—Marley was fair like their mother, Gem dark like their father—but because they were roughly the same size. It drove Gem crazy. It was why Marley had known from the age of three exactly how much older than him Gem was. She told everyone so there would be no confusion.

"What's happening?" he asked Gem, because if there ever was an instance when an older sibling came in handy, this was it.

"Why does she think she knows you?" Gem asked.

"Why does she think you're going to smite her?" Birdie asked.

"No idea," Marley said, and when he met his sister's eyes, he saw something in them he'd never seen before. Jealousy?

No way. He'd looked at her like that a lot over the years, but Marley had always thought it was a one-way street. For the first time ever, did Gem want something Marley had?

The thing in his arms?

"Do you know her, Marley?" Birdie asked.

"What *is* she?" Marley asked.

He watched a look pass between Birdie and Gem. They were sorting out whether to tell him. Or, more likely, they were sorting out whether they could get away with *not* telling him.

Not today.

"Tell me," he said, and his voice sounded different. He was a boy who had been in a fist fight.

The creature pulled back to look at Marley, which meant Marley got his first chance to look directly at it. The face was weird and wonderful, humanlike . . . yet not. It had the longest chin and two pale golden eyes that couldn't stay still. Its lips were narrow, ears pointed. And were those . . . webbed feet?

"You're so funny-looking," the creature told him. "A little scary. Not what I expected."

Marley touched his face self-consciously, wincing where he met bruised skin. "I don't always look like this."

"Marley." Birdie stepped forward. "This is Phoebe. She's a wish-granting fairy from the North Star."

Marley laughed.

"Birdie!" Gem cried. "Stop. Talking. *Now*." She turned to the other kid, the one Marley didn't know. "I can't believe her."

"Well, excuse me, but I think the fairy's already out of the bag here," Birdie said to Gem. "Besides, she *knows* Marley."

"Not just knows," the third kid said. *"Believes in."*

"Oh, and this is Van," Birdie said. "Van, Marley. Marley, Van. They found Phoebe first."

Marley noted the word *they* as his eyes ran over Van. He'd read about nonbinary kids. He'd seen a couple of TV shows. But he hadn't met a kid like Van before. It made him wonder about middle school next year and how his world would get bigger without him even doing anything different. It made him want to get there sooner.

"So you three," Marley said, studying the creature that Birdie had just referred to as a fairy, "believe in *her?*"

None of them answered right away.

Sure, it would have helped if any of them said, definitely *yes*, but Marley was also the kind of kid who could wear doubt and faith at the same time. He wasn't worried about them clashing; in fact, he liked the way they looked together. Like the Star Wars shirt and Avengers shorts that was sort of his uniform this year. He could hold this creature in his arms *and* be unsure *and* want her to be real.

"Marley?" his dad's voice shouted from upstairs.

Gem gasped, grabbed the creature, and stuffed it, writhing, inside her backpack. It occurred to Marley that his sister had taken the creature to school. Whoa.

"What's he doing home?" Gem hissed at Marley, pointing up at the ceiling in the direction of their dad's second-floor study.

"After the fight," Marley said, "they called Dad at work to pick me up."

"Perfect," Gem said, sarcastic. Then, to the others: "We need to get out of here."

They were going to leave and take the creature with them, Marley realized. His heart sank at the thought of going back to just sitting in his kitchen with his dog and his black eye.

"Mom's going to be home in twenty minutes," his dad shouted. "Be ready to tell her what happened today."

Marley groaned. It got worse. His mom was going to lose it when she heard about the fight. She was going to say awful stuff like *What happened to my sweet boy?* that made Marley want to crawl under his bed. And all the while Gem would be off with some magical being, pretending Marley didn't exist.

But then, Birdie pinched his T-shirt and gave it a little tug. "Come on."

"What? Where?"

"Crabapples. You heard your dad. You've got twenty minutes to hear what Phoebe has to say."

SIXTEEN

The Fairy's Tale

*T*was the eve of the Centennial Solstice. The night was hot, the moons were near, the meteors were mingling. All twelve hundred Wish-granters of Polaris were gathered in the quartz tree overlooking the Great Fire. At dusk, Titania, the priestess, took her place in the air. Her hair swirled past her toes, past the hem of her green gown. She whistled for quiet through her jagged teeth, then began the Children Tale.

"Fairies!" she shouted. "Elves and hobgoblins! Pixies, portunes, and sprites! Welcome!"

In the quartz boughs, hobgoblins slapped their wings. Tiny portunes danced atop the leaves, shaking tambourines. Pixie petals rained silver from the sky. Sprites lined the sacrificial platform. Elves clanged crystal gongs. The village rattled with so much anticipation, no one noticed Phoebe quaking on her low bough of honor. No one except Artemis, whose wing tip nuzzled Phoebe's.

"I'm proud of you," Artemis whispered. "When my turn comes, I'm going to be just as brave as you."

"There's still time for me to fail," Phoebe said.

"I believe in you."

"We are gathered here tonight," Titania bellowed, silencing the crowd, "to recall our bright beginning. To give thanks to our ancestors. And to praise the Child."

"Praise the Child!" came the chorus from the quartz tree, but Phoebe could not join in.

"Long ago," Titania continued, "after the human War of Ships, the Child Eriopis chose the siren Appolodorus to release her from the lowly land of Grown-Ups! She commanded Appolodorus: 'Bring me to that bright star in the Northern Sky, for there I shall be Queen.'

"And so, the siren took the Child upon her back. And as she flew, she blazed a path between Earth and our star—the river all Wishes flow through. Alas, when they arrived on Polaris, the pressures of the journey proved too much for the Child. Appolodorus laid Eriopis at the edge of our Great Fire. Her lips parted for one last breath . . . and out of her mouth marched a miracle." Titania looked at her audience, inviting the response.

"Out of the Child's mouth marched twelve new beings, the

first of the fairy kind!" came the chorus, all but Phoebe.

"We praise the Child for giving us our home! We thank her for making us Wish-granters!"

The fairies cheered again. Phoebe longed for the quiet of her Wishwell, but that was not to be. A new fairy had already been assigned her well, with its river that ran all the way to Texas.

"Tonight," Titania said, "we make our centennial sacrifice. We send one honored soul to meet the Child. Tonight, we hurl Phoebe into the Great Fire!"

"Phoebe! Phoebe! Into the Great Fire!"

Titania held out her hand. Now Phoebe was meant to fly to her. The priestess would bind Phoebe's wings and send her to her glory. But Phoebe couldn't move.

It was one thing to know that you will one day be sacrificed in the name of the Child. It was another to gaze into a fiery abyss and think, now seems like a good time. Was this really what Children wanted fairies to do? And if so, what was wrong with them?

"Come, Phoebe!" Titania said.

"Is this absolutely necessary?" Phoebe whispered to Artemis.

"Go!" Artemis kicked Phoebe off the bough with her webbed foot. Phoebe hurtled toward Titania, who caught her by the ear.

"I have questions!" Phoebe announced, facing a suddenly silent quartz tree.

"Shhh," Titania said, crisscrossing rope to bind the fairy's wings.

Phoebe spun away, slipping loose of the ties. "Are we sure the Tale is true?"

Murmurs in the boughs. Titania silenced them with a whistle. She gave Phoebe an indulgent smile. "Very sure. Very true."

"How do we know that this"—Phoebe gestured at the fire— "is what Children desire?"

"We know because we believe." Titania steered Phoebe down the glass platform, past the elves, the sprites.

"Surely we can all agree that there are holes in the Tale!" Phoebe dug her heels into the platform. The glass burned the soles of her feet. "There's no mention of what happens to me after you hurl me into the flames, and . . ." She seized Titania's hand. "What if we're wrong? What if there's no such thing as Children?"

The quartz tree gasped. Phoebe had always wondered this, but never dared say it aloud. She turned and felt the power of her question: It scared the others. It angered Titania. It thrilled Phoebe. Might there be another truth?

"Heresy," the priestess said, resuming swift knots along Phoebe's wings.

"What about my Wishes?" Phoebe cried. "I'm in the middle of granting one! In a few days, I'll be finished . . . and we can try all this again?" In the pocket of her gown, she cupped the Wish. It was small and bright. It wriggled in her palm.

"Give it to me," Titania ordered.

"Oh no."

"Give me the Wish," the priestess commanded.

It wasn't done on Polaris to take another fairy's Wish in Progress. It was a violation. And so, as Titania moved to seize the Wish, Phoebe opened her mouth. Dropped the Wish down her throat. And swallowed.

"Oops," she said, and burped.

Titania's face reddened, her eyes clouded with rage. Then she shoved the fairy off the edge of the platform. She didn't even say the blessing.

Phoebe fell toward sizzling heat, and all at once she knew: She would meet no Child on the other side. It was all a lie. Then she asked herself: Why?

With a force she'd never known before, her wings shot out. Burst free of Titania's knots. Just before the flames licked her wings, Phoebe flew over the quartz tree and its awed fairies. Over the village of glass huts. All the way to her Wishwell, where she had spent her whole existence making Wishes come true.

"PHOEBE!" Titania's voice thundered across the North Star.

Phoebe paid the priestess no mind. She needed to know where Wishes came from, and what happened once they were granted. She needed to know about Children. Were they true or not? And did they ever wonder about Fairies the way Fairies wondered about them?

She arced her wings over her head, blew a kiss for Artemis, and dove into the cool salt waters. She swam against the currents of the river, which led her to a wormhole, which spit her out in the forest halfway between Van's and Gem's front doors.

SEVENTEEN

Gem

"All that really happened?" Gem said after the fairy's tale.

"I have done the unthinkable," the fairy whispered. "I ate the Child Marley's wish."

"It was a bad wish anyway," Marley said.

"The Child is too humble," Phoebe said. "Your wish is true!"

Marley shook his head. He was looking at his feet, which made Gem wonder about his wish. How bad could it be?

"Phoebe," Van spoke up, "didn't you tell me that fairies don't see the details of the wishes they're granting? Only the . . . essence?"

Phoebe nodded. "I know the essence of Marley's wish. It's keeping me alive."

"You mean . . . ," Birdie said.

"I've been feeding off it," Phoebe said, her face full of shame.

"I think you're brave," Gem said. "You were trying to protect Marley's wish."

"I didn't want to believe," Phoebe said, near tears. "But now that I've met Marley, now that I know Children *are* true, I can't even go back to Polaris."

"Because of the fairy priestess," Van said.

Phoebe nodded. "Titania would kill me. I broke the rules—"

"But if you'd *followed* the rules, you'd be dead!" Van said. In a softer voice, they added: "I know what that feels like."

"I think a lot of kids do," Birdie said.

"I do," Marley said, touching his new black eye.

"Me too," Gem said. She was thinking of her old dance team. The one she'd quit midseason. It had killed Gem—metaphorically—even though she pretended it hadn't. She knew what it was like to be exiled from a place you used to love. She didn't want that fate for Phoebe.

Marley had his eyes closed and his face scrunched up, thinking. "Eriopis was the daughter of Jason and Medea. Jason was the leader of the Argonauts. Medea was a sorceress."

"How do you know all this?" Birdie said.

"Greek mythology was his OM team's theme last year," Gem explained, remembering the small library that had sprung up like a field of weeds in Marley's room. "He got obsessed."

"They had a bunch of kids," Marley said. "Medea murdered her sons after she and Jason had a fight. But from what I've read, no one knows what happened to Eriopis. Who's to say she didn't ride a siren to a distant star and found a colony of fairies?" He met Gem's eyes and raised a skinny shoulder. Gem was glad her brother was there.

"I'm having a hard time finding the connection," Birdie said, "between a kid who lands on a star and sprouts some fairies out of her mouth and Phoebe nearly getting tossed into a giant fireball for sport."

"But it's not sport," Gem said, "it's sacrifice. Like they used to do in the Bible or ancient Greece. Right, Marley? People did it to appease their gods."

"Kids aren't exactly gods," Van said.

Birdie laughed. Marley chuckled too. Gem wasn't sure it was so funny. Phoebe had almost died. She was still in grave shape. She was . . .

Falling on her knees before Marley?

"I've done a terrible thing," she said, bowing her head. "I await my punishment."

Try telling HER that kids aren't gods, Gem thought.

"Marley's not going to punish you, Phoebe," Birdie said.

"But I ate his wish and failed before the Great Fire—"

"No kid I know would want a fairy to sacrifice herself," Marley said.

"They . . . wouldn't?" Phoebe blinked.

Gem, Birdie, and Van shook their heads.

"When I make wishes," Marley said, "it's enough for me just to believe someone like you *might* be out there."

"You being real, Phoebe," Gem filled in. "That's already a wish come true for us."

"Let me get this straight," Phoebe said. "No Great Fire? No dead fairies? Children don't want *any* of that?"

"That's right," Van said.

"ARTEMIS!" Phoebe shouted suddenly, panicked. "My best friend. She's *next* on the sacrificial platform! At the coming Centennial Solstice. And she's not like me. She's good. She'll dive right in, unless . . ."

"You have to go back," Birdie said immediately. "You have to save her. That's what best friends do."

"I have to go back!" Phoebe pledged. "I'll face Titania. I'll do anything. Anything to save Artemis."

"How can we help?" Van asked.

"Wormholes only run in one direction, so I shall have to fly. It's a journey, but I can do it. At top gear, traveling four times the speed of light, I should get there by . . ." Phoebe broke off and whimpered. "My wings!"

"They won't work until you grant wishes again," Van said.

Phoebe nodded. "I must grant so I can fly. I must do it for Artemis." She straightened her tiny shoulders. "Well, it should be easy enough. Now that Marley is real. Now that I believe in him—"

"We're all real, Phoebe," Marley said, gesturing at Gem, at the others. "I vouch for them."

"Believe in us," Gem urged. "The more children you believe in, the more wishes you could grant, right?"

"Then you can get home," Van said.

"And save Artemis," Birdie said.

"And tell that priestess the truth about children," Gem said. "You could end the sacrifices—"

But as she spoke, Gem noticed something strange was happening to Phoebe. It was slow and subtle, but Phoebe was . . . fading. Her coloring. Her skin and her clothes, even her eyes, just *dimmed*. Her dress drained of its gold hue, her lips lost their pink, her hat muted from its dazzling red . . . until the fairy that stood before them was gray.

All different shades of gray—from her braided charcoal hair, to her dull silver skin, to her storm cloud–colored dress. It was like she had been lifted out of an old Charlie Chaplin movie.

On reflex, Gem looked down at herself. Her Nikes were still purple. There was still green ink on the back of her hand where she'd written down yesterday's science homework.

"Phoebe?" Gem said. "You okay?"

"How do you mean?"

"You turned . . . ," Van said, gesturing at their own body. "You lost your . . ."

"My wish," Marley whispered hoarsely. "Was it poison?"

Phoebe giggled sweetly, as if this was ridiculous, then looked down at herself and the tinkling sound of her laughter broke off. "Oh no. So, that's real too, I guess."

"What's real, too?" Gem asked.

"The Grays. I thought it was legend."

"What are the Grays?" Gem asked, cracking her knuckles until they hurt.

"A sickness, contracted when a fairy goes too long without granting wishes," Phoebe said. "First, her being drains of color. Then she withers. Then she dies."

"So, grant wishes!" Birdie cried. "We can make easy ones. We can do it now!"

Phoebe lay back against the trunk of the crabapple. She looked exhausted.

"I—I wish—for Gem to invite me to sleep over tonight," Birdie stammered. "So just blink your eyes or whatever, and Gem will say yes—"

"It won't work," Van said. "It needs to be a *true wish*."

"Well, where do we find one of those?" Gem cried. She

remembered Phoebe telling her in the school bathroom that wishes were shy. That they needed to feel safe to come out. But how to make a wish feel safe? Gem had no idea.

Phoebe had only just come to believe in them. Now she was going to die?

"Wait," Gem said to the fairy. "That thing you did, in Mr. Omar's class? Dropping the glamours protecting people's wishes. You could do that now. To us. Then you'd know all our true wishes—"

She looked at Phoebe, whose head was bowed, and Gem knew: The Grays had taken that power from the fairy. She was too weak now even to try.

Gem thought of Ravi Singh and his blurted-out wish about his sister. Ravi was a kid. Wouldn't granting his true wish help Phoebe? Gem almost brought it up, but something stopped her. If Phoebe did grant Ravi's wish, what would happen to his little sister? Would the girl cease to exist? That wasn't a risk they could take.

Gem's mom liked to say that everything happened for a reason. Gem didn't know if she believed that, but she did know that Phoebe had fallen into *their* lives. Van, Birdie, Gem, and now Marley, too. Together they would figure out what to do.

A jingling sound caught Gem's attention as Phoebe pushed back the sleeve of her dress, revealing a golden bracelet, heavy with charms. It gleamed against her gray skin, brighter than anything in Gem's mother's jewelry drawer, brighter than anything Gem had ever seen.

"What is that?" Gem asked.

"The true wishes of the Children of the region known as Texas," the fairy said, sliding off the bracelet, cupping it in her palm. "I'll just rest a moment, and when I wake, refreshed, I'll be ready to begin."

"Do you want a punch in the face?" Birdie asked, making it sound almost generous.

"No, no, I'll be fine."

Then, slowly, like a tired cat, the fairy began curling in on herself. Her eyes closed. Her hands pressed together, cradling her face. Her wings wrapped around her body, a silvery cocoon. Just before they came to a stop with a damp-sounding snap, the bracelet slipped from Phoebe's hand and landed in the dirt at Van's feet.

EIGHTEEN

Van

"How long should we let her sleep?" Gem asked.

"What if she doesn't wake up?" Marley asked.

"What if she's already dead?" Birdie asked.

"Don't say that!" Gem said.

"Do you think she dropped the bracelet on purpose?" Van asked. "For us?"

For a moment, they were quiet. Then Gem shook her head. "She said she'd start granting wishes once she woke up."

"If she were well enough to do that," Birdie said, "don't you think she would have already?"

"I think we should help her," Van said. "Her friend's

in danger, and we don't know how much time we have, how often these Centennial Solstices take place in her star system."

"But we also have no idea how the bracelet works," Gem said.

"We have no idea how it works *yet* . . ." Van picked up the bracelet. They couldn't believe how heavy it was, how many charms it held. There must have been thousands of them, tiny intricate golden baubles, each representing a wish. Each belonging to a kid.

Fine details were etched into the gold. There was a snake with a diamond pattern on its scales. A key that looked like it could open a very tiny door. A pine tree with detailed needles, a cloud with a fluffy texture, a rose with a dense whorl of petals. There was a pair of dice, a near-perfect miniature of the one that came with Van's Monopoly board.

Van thought about the student body at Wonder Middle School, all the people they hadn't made friends with this year. Kids they'd written off for various offenses. Too mean, too straight, too self-absorbed. They'd done it without realizing, because it was easier than carrying all that rejection on their back. But something about this bracelet, these charms, made Van feel for all those kids they'd never liked. It made them seem more human.

They sat down and fished through the charms. The

others joined them in a circle around Phoebe. And then, in the midst of that jumble of gold, Van saw the dart.

They held it between their fingers to study it. The three-pronged flight, the narrow shaft and crosshatched barrel, the point so sharp Van pricked themself, sucking in their breath. So much like Caro's dart, the one inside Van's jumpsuit pocket. A funny feeling came over them. It was a good feeling. A sureness. Like they were doing something right.

"Van?" Gem said.

"I think . . ." They felt a tremor in their hand as they tugged lightly at the dart.

It slipped off the chain.

The others gasped. At first, Van thought they'd broken the bracelet. But then, they discovered two things:

First, the bracelet was still intact, the other charms all still bound by their golden band.

Second, when Van had plucked the dart free, a second chain had appeared, grown out of the dart's flight.

There were now two golden bracelets. The original with thousands of charms—and a second, larger chain with one. Van sensed that the dart chain was theirs. *Their wish?* Could it be?

They glanced at the fairy, so gray, so still. Should they be doing this?

They were trying to help, Van told themself. They were trying to save Phoebe.

They didn't know much about jewelry, but they thought chains usually had clasps. This one didn't. So how would someone put it on? Van wanted to. They tried sliding it over their fingers, down to the palm of their hand. At the moment they expected it to get stuck, the gold links gave, stretching to slide over the wide part of their palm. The bracelet settled on their wrist. It fit.

"How did you do that?" Gem asked.

"I think it's mine," Van said.

"It's an arrow?" Marley asked.

"I don't know," Van lied. "I'm not sure what it means." There was much Van didn't know about the bracelet, but they were sure it represented Caro's dart. They weren't sure why they didn't want to admit this to the others. They held out the bracelet, hoping someone else would take the spotlight off them.

"I can't even think of anything I've wished for recently," Gem said, hugging her knees.

"Well, yesterday you *did* wish you'd never been born," Birdie quipped.

Gem glared at her. "Why do you go out of your way to hurt my feelings?"

"I don't!" Birdie said, looking shocked. "I thought you'd laugh. I didn't mean—Gem, I'm sorry—"

"You don't take anything that matters to me seriously!"

"I take everything about you *so* seriously!" Birdie said,

like she was swearing an oath. "But you barely share anything with me anymore. I had to find out from Ava Rhodes that you quit the dance team!"

"I didn't feel like talking about it." Gem looked down. "You don't know what it's like."

"I would have listened." Birdie's voice wavered, and Van wondered if she might cry. "I would have tried to understand."

Van felt awkward. If they weren't in the middle of divvying up golden wishes, Van would leave. Give Gem and Birdie some privacy.

"There's your charm, Gem," Birdie said darkly, dropping the bracelet into Gem's lap. "The golden rose you always wanted."

"Of course!" Marley said. "Gem, from your dance team."

"No," Gem said, and pushed the bracelet away.

"Wait, what does the rose have to do with Gem's dance team?" Van asked.

"*Ex*–dance team," Gem said.

"The Golden Rose is really special," Marley said. "It's a trophy given to the sixth-grade girl on Gem's dance team who performs a solo in the recital."

"And I quit dance a couple of months ago," Gem said.

"But still," Van said, "chances are, that one is yours."

"It's *not* my wish," Gem said.

"Fine," Birdie said sarcastically. "Let's see if it's mine." She took the bracelet, held the rose between her fingers, and tugged. Nothing happened. She tugged again.

"Don't break it!" Gem cried, and reached for the bracelet herself. As she did, her fingers just seemed to *find* the golden rose. It slipped off the chain so easily, forming its own new chain, just as Van's had.

Now Gem had the rose, but she didn't look happy about it. To Van's mind, they were making progress. They were figuring this out. What if they could identify each of their wishes before Phoebe woke up? Surely it would help her.

"I'm always the last one," Birdie muttered to herself, tugging on the different charms.

"You'll find it," Gem said, her voice kinder now.

"Maybe I'm not part of this. Maybe it's just for y'all."

"Don't just guess, Birdie," Gem said. "Focus."

"You've got this, Birdie," Van said.

Birdie's fingers hovered, then wrapped around the pine-tree charm. She took a deep breath and closed her eyes. She pulled and the charm loosened, slipped off.

Van clapped. Marley whooped. Gem put her arms around Birdie.

"What does it mean?" Gem asked.

Birdie chewed her lip. "I—I don't know."

Van studied their charm and thought about Caro. Of course they wished they were back in Ireland with their best friend and former life, but for the thousandth time, there wasn't anything they could do about it. So that couldn't be what the dart meant. Why was it so hard to find one true wish? Fingering the charm, Van already felt like they were letting Phoebe down. They dropped the dart. It clanged against their watch—which told Van, unfortunately, that they were late for their flute lesson.

It was hard to believe that two things as opposite as hiding a fairy in the crabapples and Van's regular Wednesday Zoom flute lesson could exist in the same realm, but this was Van's life now.

"Marlowe Thelonious Cash!" a woman's voice bellowed beyond the crabapples.

"Mom's home," Gem said to Marley.

"I'm toast," he groaned.

"I have to go too," Van said.

"Wait," Gem said, reaching for Van at the gap in the boughs. "We need a plan. Tonight, each of us needs to figure out what wish our charms represent."

Van swallowed. "I'll try."

"It'll help to make your wish feel . . . safe," Gem said.

"Safe?" Van asked. "What does that mean?"

"I don't know. It's probably different for each wish. Just give it a try," Gem said.

Marley was tucking the bracelet under the sleeping fairy's wing, smoothing the folds of her dress. "What about Phoebe? Shouldn't we take her inside? I could make her a bed under the—"

"No," Van, Birdie, and Gem all said at once.

"She needs a view of the stars," Van said.

"And zero snooping parents," Gem said.

"She was okay here last night," Birdie said.

"You left her *here*? Alone?" Marley asked, horrified.

"It's the safest place," Van said, though they hated to leave the fairy too. They had barely slept the night before, worrying whether Phoebe was comfortable, was safe.

"I still can't believe we took her out of the crabapples to go to school," Birdie said. "And got away with it."

"We need to be more careful," Gem said, "especially now that she's sick."

"She's our secret," Van said.

"And she needs to stay that way," Birdie added.

"From now on," Gem said, looking at each of them in turn, "we *don't* take her beyond the crabapples. And we don't let anyone else in."

Gem put her hand out. Birdie put her hand atop it. Marley did the same. Van stepped forward and completed the circle, adding their hand. They squeezed.

A pact.

"And tomorrow?" Van said.

"Tomorrow we meet back here," Gem said. "Bring your true wish, and cross your fingers that Phoebe's up for granting."

Nineteen

Birdie

In English the next day, Birdie sketched pine trees in the margins of her notebook until her writing assessment looked like the stationery Gem brought home from Camp Evergreen.

Why couldn't Birdie have made a different wish? Why did this have to be the one that Phoebe's life depended on?

Birdie's wish was to go to Camp Evergreen with Gem. She'd known it from the moment she'd touched the charm in the crabapples yesterday. She'd lied to the others and acted confused, but Birdie had been wishing for the same thing for years. Her wish had never felt so critical as it did this year. Her friendship with Gem was on life support, and if Gem left for six weeks, Birdie feared that when she came back, it would be declared officially dead.

Still, sleepaway camp was so far out of her parents' budget that Birdie might as well have wished for a Lamborghini or a trip to space. Even if Phoebe was able to grant Birdie's family several thousand extra dollars—which didn't seem like the kind of thing magical fairies wasted their magical time on—Birdie's parents would probably spend it on something boring like a washing machine. And Birdie's wish would remain a useless golden charm forever.

The worst part was: Camp Evergreen was just a front for what Birdie really wanted. She wanted things between her and Gem not to suck so much. She'd convinced herself that camp would solve their problems. But recently, Birdie didn't even know if that was true.

This year, there were all these obstacles popping up out of nowhere between Birdie and Gem. Things that Gem had and Birdie didn't, things that led Gem to say stuff like *You don't know what it's like.*

The words stung because they were true. They made Birdie feel small and weak, like she sucked at being a best friend, and probably a human.

In class, Ms. Sae Tang wrote on the board:

Two Important Questions the Writer Must Ask:
What does my character want?
What stands in their way of getting it?

Birdie drew another pine tree in the margins. And then, instead of the prompt she was supposed to be answering using the second-person point of view, Birdie wrote:

What I Want:

Go back to normal with Gem

Camp Evergreen

In My Way:

Period

Boobs

Pit hair

Thousands of dollars to pay for camp

She was trying to figure out how to tackle a single one of these insurmountable obstacles when Ms. Sae Tang crossed behind her desk and leaned over to look at Birdie's paper.

"Birdie—"

Birdie knew that whatever was about to happen was too embarrassing to survive, so she did the only thing she could think to do. She created a distraction. She jumped up from her desk, reached behind her for the wall, and pulled the fire alarm.

An hour of detention, a super-fun chat with the fire chief, and an atomic bomb of a lecture from her mother later, Birdie was popping out the screen of her bedroom window, climbing through it, and mounting her bike.

She'd waited until her mom logged on to an hour-long Zoom Pilates class in her bedroom. The class cost twelve dollars, so Birdie knew her mother wouldn't come out, even if their house had a fire alarm for Birdie to pull. Which meant that, although Birdie was technically grounded, she had exactly fifty-seven minutes to make it to the crabapples and back.

She booked the three miles to Gem's block. She practically barreled into the crabapples, where Marley, Gem, and Van were all sitting so quietly it made Birdie feel crazy. She felt like a clown crashing a study hall.

"Birdie!" Van said. "You made it!"

"Did you seriously pull the fire alarm?" Gem asked.

"Birdie probably had a good reason for doing it," Marley said, and waved her over.

Birdie remembered Ms. Sae Tang's expression right after she pulled the alarm—her arms held out at her sides, like *Why?* Did doing something stupid to cover up doing something mortifying count as a good reason? Birdie didn't feel like getting into it.

"How is she?" Birdie nodded toward Phoebe.

"Worse," Gem said. "She won't even wake up for tea."

Birdie's heart swelled at the sight of the motionless gray cocoon. Gone was her fear that she'd be found out as the reason Phoebe came to Texas. There was so much more at stake now than Birdie's silly pride.

"Is she still . . . breathing?" Birdie asked.

"Breathing? Yes," Van said. "In a state to grant wishes? Not so much." They glanced at Gem, and Birdie got the feeling a decision had been reached before she got there.

"We're going to have to do it ourselves," Gem said.

"Do what?"

"Grant our own wishes," Van said.

Birdie laughed. It was . . . ridiculous. She was eleven years old.

"We may not have a choice," Van said, glancing at Phoebe's pitiful cocoon.

"You're serious?" Birdie said. "But . . . how? I can't even remember to feed my goldfish half the time. Doesn't granting wishes require magic? Last time I checked, I don't have any."

Birdie thought she'd made her case, but the others were staring at her, even Marley, like they were waiting for her to catch up. She swallowed. And then, she decided to try.

Phoebe needed them. She was their cause now, and Birdie threw herself into her causes. So what if it was impossible? Had Gem given Birdie that mug for her birthday with the *Alice in Wonderland* quote "Do Six Impossible Things Before Breakfast" for nothing? Birdie didn't think so.

"All right," she said. "Let's grant."

"Yes!" Gem said. "So, who's first?"

There was quiet in the crabapples. Birdie cleared her throat. She would tell them about Camp Evergreen. She'd just come out with the whole thing.

But when she looked at Gem, her eyebrows started sweating at the thought of saying it aloud. She would do it in a minute.

"Did you figure out your charms?" she asked Gem and Van, twirling her own between her fingers, stalling.

"Not exactly," Van said. "Gem doesn't want anything to do with that dance recital."

"What about your arrow?" Birdie asked, and noticed Van looking away. It made her wonder whether, like Birdie, Van had more of an idea about their charm than they'd let on.

"On the bright side," Van said, changing the subject, "Marley figured out how much time we have to get Phoebe home."

"Seriously?" Birdie looked at Marley, hunched over a giant astronomy textbook that looked like it was for a college student.

"My theory is that the fairy concept of Centennial Solstice probably refers to the day Polaris will most closely align with our North Celestial Pole."

"Which is when?" Birdie asked.

"March 24th, 2100."

"So, we have a little time?" Birdie joked.

"*Little* being the operative word," Marley said. "Phoebe said she can travel at top speed at four times the speed of light . . . so, according to my calculations"—he swallowed—"she has until next Saturday around twilight to lift off again and get home in time to save Artemis."

"Just what we need," Birdie said, "a ticking clock."

She flopped down next to Gem, her eyes falling on Gem's brainstorming notes about roses . . . written on Camp Evergreen stationery. Okay, this was a sign. Birdie took a deep breath.

She slipped the gold chain off her wrist, placed the pine-tree charm over the printed tree on Gem's paper. She met Gem's eyes and tried to smile normally, like she wasn't nervous.

"So. I think I . . . sorta . . . wished to go to camp?"

"Really? That's great!" Van said, coming to study Birdie's charm. "Camp is easy. Camp we can grant—"

Birdie shook her head. "No. Not easy. My parents can't afford it. Not even close. I've begged my mom for years, but . . ."

"You know they have scholarships, right?" Marley said.

Birdie looked at Marley. She blinked. "Scholarships?"

"There's an application online. They're project-based, like you think of something you can offer to the camp. Last year, our photographer was there on scholarship. Remember, Gem? He made this cool yearbook."

Birdie looked at Gem. Of all the stories Gem came home with last summer, the origins of the yearbook she painstakingly pored over had not been one Birdie had heard. Birdie felt cold and hot at once—cold on her arms, blazing in her head. And she suddenly realized that the only person who hadn't yet said a word about Birdie's wish was Gem.

"Gem?"

"Your *true wish* is *camp*?" Gem said, and laughed in a way that punched Birdie in the gut. "At least I'm not the only one who wasted a wish on something pathetic."

If there was a moment for truth, this was it. Birdie should have said that camp wasn't pathetic, not at all. Not unless Gem thought saving their friendship was pathetic. She should have said that what mattered to Birdie most in the world was her bond with Gem. And that she felt it breaking. And that she was scared. And that she'd give anything to fix it. And that all of that big, complicated stuff somehow got wrapped up into one efficient word, *camp*.

But Birdie found she couldn't say any of that. She found those words felt way too risky. So what she said instead was:

"You've known all this time Camp Evergreen offered scholarships? You've known how much I wanted to go? Every single year, Gem? And you've never even mentioned it?"

"Birdie—" Gem started to say, but Birdie waved her off. Her mom would be finished with Pilates soon, and this—whatever was happening here—was not worth getting double grounded for. It's not like they were going to fix Phoebe by next Saturday anyway, so what was the point? Even if they did, who was to say Phoebe's friendship with this Artemis character was worth the effort? Not all friendships were. . . .

"I'm out," Birdie said, and she grabbed her bike and left.

TWENTY

Van

When Van's mam came home from her shift at the dry cleaners, she always watched her favorite Irish talk show, the *Late Late Show*, on her laptop in the living room before she went in to make dinner. She said that Tubs, the show's host, was the one thing she'd never quit about Ireland.

It was like Mam to pick the lightest, most insignificant piece of their former life and hold on to it like a dog to a bone. The things about Ireland that Van didn't want to quit—friends, confidence, the ability to make jokes that people laughed at—couldn't be streamed online.

They wondered if they'd ever make Gem or Birdie

laugh. They wondered, once they sorted out Phoebe's troubles, if they'd even see Gem and Birdie outside school.

They wondered if Gem and Birdie would want to see *each other* outside school after today. If Van knew the girls better, they would have tried to mediate when the camp conversation got hot. But they didn't. So they hadn't.

Van fingered the dart charm up their sleeve as Mam settled onto the couch. They checked their phone for the eight hundredth time, but Caro hadn't written back. If they'd met Phoebe back home, Caro would have Van's wish sorted and granted before it was time for tea. But an ocean away, Van didn't even know how to broach the subject with their friend. Even if they did know, Caro wasn't writing back.

"Who's on tonight?" they asked Mam, pointing at the screen.

"Oh, that hilarious gal. The one from the . . . you know . . . ah, we watched it together." She patted the cushion for Van to join her on the couch. "I'm so tired, love. And my feet."

"Let's see them," Van said.

Mam propped her legs on Van's lap on the couch. Leaning back against the cushions, making sure the dart-charm chain was hidden up their sleeve, they set to work. They pressed their thumbs into the soles of Mam's feet. They went through the nightly massage as they watched

Tubs crack his usual jokes about the prime minister.

Van knew how to massage because of Mam, who used to work in a fancy spa at a fancy inn outside Dublin. If she missed the work she used to be known for, had once been written up in a magazine for, if she felt the drop in career fulfillment since she'd taken the first job she could get in Texas at the dry cleaners, she didn't complain about it to Van.

Van wouldn't have minded if Mam did complain once in a while. Then at least they wouldn't be the only one.

"What have you been into that made your hands so dirty?" Mam said. "You could grow spuds under those nails."

"I was outside, at the . . ." They needed to talk to Mam about Phoebe, but even though they'd spent the past few hours knowing this, they had no idea where to begin.

"My child, *outside*? Are you feeling all right?" She put a hand to Van's forehead teasingly, and Van leaned into her touch. They were close with their mam, could get a hug anytime, so why didn't they want her to take her hand off their head tonight?

It was just that the days were so lonely here. In Ireland, anytime they weren't in desks or orchestra chairs, Van and their friends were piled up in a heap of arms and legs and shoulders anyone could lay their head on. The group hug, they called it, and Van fed on it. They hadn't realized how much until there was no friend to touch anymore. The closest they'd come to hugging a kid in Texas was when they'd tried to tackle Birdie to keep her from seeing Phoebe.

Mam moved her hand down from Van's forehead to cup their cheek. She looked like she was about to ask Van whether they were all right, so Van cut her off at the pass.

"I know," they said. "You're going to tell me how, when you were young, you stayed outdoors all hours until Gran rang that bell."

"'Twas the fairy curfew," Mam said with a nod.

"The . . . what?" Van said, sitting straighter. Fairy lore peppered their youth so much that it blended together with the rest of the regular tales, but they didn't remember this one.

"I've told you about it," Mam said. "It's silly, I know, and you were never interested in such—"

"I'm interested now," Van said. "Tell me."

"Well, you know Gran claimed she saw the fairies all her life. Most of us, my generation, used to swear we saw them as children. 'Course, I never really did." She laughed. "But Gran fancied she saw them right until the end. She said she knew their ways." Their mam paused a moment, reminiscing. "The bell didn't mean tea—it meant the sky was right for fairies, so in we ran to safety."

"Because the fairies were dangerous?" Van asked.

"Dangerous, vengeful, unpredictable. Gran kept iron over all the entries to the house. Horseshoes over the door, the poker by the fire. She said the fairies hate iron."

"What do fairies like?" Van said, trying to keep their voice subdued, like they were barely interested, humoring their mam. Like they didn't have just nine days to save Phoebe.

"You mean the rare nice ones? The ones we'd try to coax out from their glens?"

"Those ones, yes."

"Ah, the usual, I suppose. Dancing. Music."

That would explain the trance that Phoebe had fallen into during orchestra the day before.

"The colors of flowers," their mam continued. "Pinks and reds and greens. You don't remember this, but as a babe, you used to dance naked with your cousins in many a fairy circle."

"Kind of you to remind me."

Van knew Birdie and Gem and Marley would be stunned by this conversation, but in Ireland, the topic of fairies came up more often than it did in Texas. Even if most Irish people thought fairy lore was only fancy, there were the true believers like Van's gran. Now Van was realizing how much wisdom lived in Gran's old stories.

They wished Gran was still here. They wished they'd paid more attention to her fairy tales when they were young.

"I miss Gran," Van said.

"Me too."

"I miss home. Can't we go this summer?"

"It's out of the question, Van. I don't have the money, and your da's taking you—"

Van groaned to cut her off. "Hawaii."

"Yes. To horrible Hawaii," Mam said in a distant voice that made Van feel guilty. They were quiet for a moment in the awkward way that only the topic of Van's da could bring on.

"I just mean it'll be lonely," Van said.

"I know, love." Mam took one of their hands and studied their fingernails. "Is that what you're out there doing, trying to coax a fairy friend from the forest near your da's house?"

Van held their breath, wondering how Mam could be so perceptive . . . and then they realized that Mam didn't mean it. She thought, if anything, Van was out there playing pretend. Alone.

"You know," Mam said, "a fairy friend is never so good as a real human one."

"I have some of those," Van said as the laptop screen went to commercial.

"You do, now?" Mam closed the computer and looked at Van. "And what are their names?"

"Birdie," Van said, looking away. "And Gem. And Marley."

"That Birdie down the street? The speeding bicyclist?"

"The very one." Van smiled.

"Good," Mam said. "And are they kind to you?"

Van wondered if she'd ask this question if Van weren't nonbinary, or maybe if this town weren't so binary. They decided yes, that kindness mattered to their mam, no matter who or where you were.

They thought of Birdie complimenting their sketches. They thought of Gem helping them up off the ground before they'd even been introduced. They thought of Marley, who was kind to everyone by nature. They told the truth: "They are."

Mam nodded. "I'm glad to hear it. And I know you're kind to them."

Van nuzzled closer to Mam. They lifted the screen of the laptop, because the commercial would be over, and the musical guest on soon, because if they kept talking like this, it might get embarrassing. This conversation had been good. It had left Van and Mam feeling close.

Mam laughed at the show some more, but Van was deep in thought. Music and dancing and iron and curfews. On some level, they knew all these things, but they were buried down deep, and it had helped to have their mum excavate a few. They would tell the others tomorrow.

They thought of Birdie suddenly, pedaling her bike away in anger. Mam hadn't asked if these new friends were kind to each other. Did it matter, Van wondered?

Couldn't they still help Phoebe, even if Gem and Birdie were fighting? Van and Caro used to fight sometimes— over what to do on the weekend, or whether a show was heteronormative. But nothing like Birdie and Gem, who it sometimes seemed could barely stand to be around each other. In the short time Van had seen them up close, their friendship seemed . . . sick.

Just like Phoebe seemed sick.

Was it possible Gem and Birdie's problems were threatening the fairy's life?

TWENTY-ONE

Gem

When Gem got to the crabapples on Friday after school, Van was already there. They were sitting next to Phoebe's cocoon with their flute case on their lap.

"I didn't know if anyone was coming," Gem said. "Marley has OM and . . ."

"Birdie?" Van said.

"She had something to do."

This was what Birdie had told Gem, but Gem didn't believe it. She knew Birdie's schedule—newspaper on Mondays, but every other day, especially now that Gem had quit dance, Birdie came home with Gem.

Birdie had had "something to do" at lunch that day too,

even after Gem slipped her a note between first and second period apologizing for what she'd said about Birdie's wish. During lunch, Gem had hung around the wall for four minutes, thinking maybe Van would show up. But they hadn't, and Gem started to feel the handball kids' eyes on her, standing there alone like she didn't have a friend, so she'd gone inside and sat at Ava Rhodes's table and wished to be here instead.

Now she *was* here, and Phoebe looked worse than when they'd left her the day before. She was grayer still and shallow of breath in her sleep.

"What if we can't help her in time?" Gem asked quietly.

"We have to," Van said. "So we will."

Gem nodded, though if Birdie had said the exact same thing, Gem would have challenged her. It would have become a fight. And for what?

"Van?" she said. "Do you think I'm mean?"

Van looked at her. Van took their time answering. Gem prepared for the worst. If she were to ask another kid this, say Ava Rhodes or one of her friends, the question wouldn't even be off Gem's lips before the girl denied it. Then they'd start talking about who made Gem feel mean, and how mean *that* kid was, so long as they weren't within earshot. And it would have less to do with Gem actually being mean or nice, and more to do with how most kids wouldn't miss a chance to talk behind someone else's back.

Finally Van said, "I don't think you're mean. But I don't think Birdie's mean either."

And just like that, they wouldn't be talking about Birdie behind her back. Gem realized she was grateful.

Van unclasped their flute case, fit the pieces together. "I was talking to my mam last night. Her mam, my gran, knew a lot about fairies."

"You told your mom?" Gem was shocked. Part of her was dying to tell her own mother everything going on under the crabapples, but the other part of her knew it was a secret.

To Gem's relief, Van shook their head. "No, but Gran used to talk about fairies like she talked about the weather. Mam and I grew up on the tales. She reminded me how fairies love music. And dancing. So I brought my flute."

"Well, I'm not dancing," Gem said, crossing her arms.

"That's all right." Van shrugged and brought the flute to their lips. But before they played a note, they asked, "Why'd you quit?"

"Because I hate it."

The words came automatically. It was what she'd told her parents, Coach, and anyone else who asked. It was her story. She'd stuck to it. Through the baffled phone calls with her mom and Coach. Through two extremely useless sessions with some therapist friend of her dad. Always Gem insisted she didn't have anything more to say.

"I saw you perform at the Christmas market thing," Van said. "At the mall. You're really good. I guess everyone tells you that."

Gem glanced at Van, their short hair and brown T-shirt and jeans and glasses and flute. It occurred to her that, out of anyone she knew, Van might actually *get* it. The truth.

And so, for the first time, Gem decided to tell it.

"Last month, Coach posted our recital costumes," she said. "It's a big day. Everyone gets excited. She tacks up pictures from this catalog on a board so the whole team can see." Gem swallowed, saw the board in her mind. "I have a solo this year. *Had* a solo. But my costume . . ."

Her voice hitched, and a lump formed in her throat. She couldn't explain how Coach expected her to wear basically a *bra* and miniskirt. While leaping around. Onstage. In front of hundreds of people.

"You'd rather die than wear it?" Van said.

That was it. She would rather die than wear it.

Gem meant to nod, but what happened was that she broke down and cried. Big sobs came out of her, and Van scooted over in the dirt and held her in a hug. She shook and cried and couldn't believe how much there was to let out.

After a while, though, Gem started to feel scared. She and Van barely knew each other, and now her snot was all over Van's shirt. Did Gem seem super weird or what?

"Sorry." Gem pulled away and wiped her eyes.

"Don't be. Thanks for telling me," Van said, which was nice, even if they probably didn't mean it. "You miss it, though? I mean, forget the costume. Just . . . dancing?"

It might have been easier if Van was just being nice. But the truth was: Van understood her. Not just because of Gem's discomfort over her costume. Because Van was a musician. And when something like that got in you, Gem knew, Van knew, it was *in* you. Deep and always.

"Yeah," Gem admitted. "But not enough to go back." She gestured at Phoebe. She felt like she might cry again. "I don't know what to do about my wish. If it means the difference between saving her and . . ."

"No," Van said. "There would be nothing 'true' about you wearing something that makes you feel bad in order to get some trophy."

"Which means it wouldn't help Phoebe, either," Gem said glumly.

"Gem, why can't you just wear something else?"

"It doesn't work that way. Coach—" She broke off, looked at Van, the kid who'd said, in a lot of very big ways: *Screw the way things work.*

It was inspiring.

"I never even asked Coach," Gem said. "Even if I thought wearing something else was an option, I was too embarrassed to ask."

"Do it now," Van said. "Do it for Phoebe."

Gem tried to imagine speaking up about her body, about what she was comfortable putting on it. And what she was not comfortable with. It *terrified* her. More than scorpions. She could already feel every muscle tensing. She avoided the topic of her body like the plague. To have to explain what her boobs would do in that bra-thing . . .

But then she tried to imagine herself dancing. In her imagination, she didn't bother with what she was wearing. She was moving to the steps she had choreographed herself, triple pirouettes and grand jetés across the floor, to music she had listened to a thousand times and never got sick of. She was doing what she loved.

What if she sent Coach an email?

"I could help," Van said, and smiled at her.

Gem smiled back. It had felt okay to tell the truth, to have someone hear it and not laugh, not even look at her weird. She felt a little looser.

Van picked up their flute. They began to play a melody that made Gem think of climbing. It sounded like something Gem would hear on her dad's classical radio station. Van was *good*, and not just for a kid. It was beautiful. It was music Gem could dance to.

She looked at Phoebe. The fairy was still, but Gem got the feeling she was listening.

Gem had been dancing all her life. Even in line buying

gum at the gas station, if a good song came on, Gem would twirl. Before she knew it, she was on her feet now.

She didn't think about what kind of dancing a fairy would like. She knew. The same way she knew the shape that Van's song would take. She extended her arms, raised her chin. She let her heart lead her as she spun and leapt around the crabapples. All the way until Van's flute trilled a long, high final note and someone started clapping.

Gem turned to find Phoebe awake. She was still gray, but her wings were drawn back now. She was applauding. She was watching Gem and smiling.

"Teach me how to do that?"

Twenty-Two

Birdie

Birdie," Mr. Chatterjee said from door of the journalism room. "I've got to lock up. My cats get separation anxiety if I'm not home by the time *Kelly Clarkson* is over."

"I'm done," Birdie called, taking the warm final page from the printer. "Thanks for letting me use the Beast, Mr. C."

Birdie had a love-hate relationship with the journalism printer. They'd been through twenty-seven issues of the *Wonder Gazette* this year, and about quadruple that number of paper jams. But today the Beast had come through for her, and Birdie held the proof in her hands. She tucked the mock-up into her backpack, elbow-bumped Mr. C on her way out the door, and started jogging for her bike.

"Give the cats a scratch for me," she called over her shoulder.

Birdie liked leaving school when it was empty—no buses to dodge, no car line to jockey past, no other kids waging silent wars with her on their own bikes. Just Birdie and the blue sky and the whir of her wheels over pavement. But as she pedaled toward the crabapples, the lightness she'd felt in her chest leaving school became heavier. She was proud of what she'd just done, but it wasn't that simple. Now she had to show Gem.

She dumped her bike on the Cashes' lawn next to Gem's old Schwinn. She noticed another bike parked upright and actually using its kickstand. Van's. So they were here. Together already. Without her. Okay.

As she started for the crabapples, her mood souring like the milk on her cereal that morning, Birdie spotted a cloaked figure creeping out the Cashes' side window.

"Psst. Marley," she whispered as he dropped to the ground in a crouch. She squinted. "Is that a Robin Hood costume?"

"Closest thing I have to camo," he whispered. "I'm still grounded, but I need to see her."

Birdie nodded. She, too, needed to see Phoebe. She, too, was still grounded. Luckily, her parents worked late on Fridays. She took a recon glance around the yard for Marley.

"Coast's clear."

"What's that?" Marley asked, pointing at Birdie's papers as they headed for the cul-de-sac.

"What's *that*?" Birdie asked, gesturing at the sound of music coming from the crabapples.

A second later, she and Marley were through the boughs. Phoebe was awake! She was standing! She, Gem, and Van were . . . facing a phone and learning the moves to a TikTok dance? What had Birdie missed?

"Hey!" Gem said at the sight of them. Her cheeks were pink, her feet moving fast beneath her. She smiled. Automatically, Birdie smiled back, feeling it spread through her, down to her toes. Amazing how fast she and Gem could get back to good. Sometimes all it took was a smile.

"Hey," Birdie said. "What's up?"

"We're showing Phoebe how to do the Willow. Try it."

"When did she wake up?" Birdie asked, falling in line even though the moves were way beyond her. She tried to do some stuff with her arms that looked halfway like what Gem was doing. Fail. Van was pretty pathetic too, but they still seemed to be having fun.

As Birdie watched Gem lead the choreography, it crossed her mind that maybe this was connected to Gem's wish—something about being able to dance without having to be on that dumb team that took up all her time? To be free and still a dancer? That'd be a pretty good wish.

Was that why Phoebe was awake and looking less close to death's door?

"How are you feeling, Phoebe?" Marley asked.

"Better," she said, but her weak voice tugged at Birdie's heart.

"What about your wings?" Birdie asked her.

"Still busted," Van said as Phoebe twitched her wings dejectedly. "But we told her about our charms, our plan to help grant our own wishes. She's into it."

"Usually, I work alone," Phoebe said. "But to save Artemis, I'll take all the help I can get."

Birdie nodded. "Speaking of which. I've got news. Literally."

"What is it?" Van asked.

The others gathered around her as Birdie pulled out her work in progress. "My application for a scholarship to camp."

The Evergreen Editorial

A new periodical by Birdie B

Sveiki Stovyklautojai! That's *Hello Campers* in Lithuanian, which is my family's native tongue. I'm Birdie B, your friendly new Evergreen editor, and this week's issue is dedicated to the best part of camp . . . YOU.

I'm new around here and excited to get to know y'all. But what exactly makes y'all y'all? Is it a secret skill you'll show off at Wednesday's talent show? (Add your name to the sign-up sheet today.) Or maybe it's your heritage? (I've never been to Lithuania, but I follow some Lithuanian bloggers and know all the cake shops I want to visit.) Is it your friendships that define you? (Don't sleep on this week's camper spotlight, p. 6!)

I can't wait to find out what makes you you this summer. And if you want to learn any more Lithuanian catchphrases, you know where to find me.

Ever(green) yours,

Birdie B

Page two of the newsletter featured Birdie's latest comic, *From the Well of Phoebe LaCroix*. In five panels, she had sketched her fairy villain packing for camp, cooking up hilarious and destructive schemes to unleash upon the campers. The last panel showed Phoebe diving through her wishing well on the North Star, with the caption, *Evergreen or buuuuuuust!*

Birdie had written other sections, taking inspiration from some of the *Wonder Gazette*'s most successful columns—a Trends Watch, a Joke of the Day, a summary of the week's news headlines. But the last feature was the one she'd worked hardest on, and was most nervous about:

Spotlight on: Gem Cash

Gemima (Gem) Cash—she/her—is a six-year veteran of Camp Evergreen and a top-bunker in the Sequoia Cabin this summer. She hails from Lewisville, Texas, where she attends Wonder Middle School as a rising seventh grader. She has one sibling (Marley—he/him, bottom-bunker in the Pine Cabin), one dog (Groovy), and one crazy grandma who rides a motorcycle (Honda Shadow). Gem's favorite movie is *Beaches*, her favorite book is *Genesis Begins Again*, and her favorite YouTube channel is Cook with Amber. She excels at Scrabble, macramé, world history, giving advice, burning cookies, remembering birthdays, and smiling.

Full disclosure: Gem is best friends with Birdie B, and nothing will ever change that.

"Birdie," Marley said when he came to the end. "You did it."

"How did you know?" Phoebe asked, staring at the comic panels. "How do you know my well so well?"

Birdie was thinking of how to answer Phoebe when

Gem suddenly closed her in a hug. Birdie held her breath. Hugged back.

"Thanks for what you wrote about me."

"It's a rough draft," Birdie said. "I can add dancing to your 'excels at' list. I went back and forth."

"That'd be good," Gem said, and smiled. She handed Birdie back the paper. "How did you know all these details—the names of the cabins? The Wednesday night talent shows?"

"My Wishwell?" Phoebe said.

Birdie looked at her shoes. "I just paid attention. And remembered."

"Mr. Garcia is going to love this," Gem said.

"You think?" Birdie's heart lifted. Gem's parents were friends with the camp director of Evergreen. Sometimes they went to his house for game night. Gem had the kind of intel that Birdie needed on what might impress her target audience.

Gem nodded, looked Birdie in the eye, and grinned Birdie's favorite grin in the galaxy. "You're going to be the first to make their wish come true."

TWENTY-THREE

Van

Van: Can you two come over Sunday afternoon?

Birdie: . . .

Gem: Sure, what's up?

Birdie: Yup

Van: I have a plan for gem's wish and need more hands.

We'll have the house to ourselves until three. Tell marley?

I don't have his number

Birdie: See ya then

Van was more nervous about having the others over than they'd been on the first day of school. They'd put on the kettle and got out the good tin of biscuits that Mam kept on top of the fridge. They'd even made their bed. If only Mam's sewing machine didn't weigh a trillion kilos, they would have hauled it to the crabapples, so that they could sew with Phoebe nearby. But they would visit the fairy after the costume was complete, once they were closer to granting Gem's wish.

At eleven fifteen, Van's phone buzzed. Racing for it, they convinced themself it was Birdie or Gem saying they couldn't come. But it was Caro's face on the screen. Van had messaged them several times this week, but between school and the time difference, it was nearly impossible to connect. Finally they could ask Caro about the dart . . . only just then, the doorbell rang. And Van had to choose: Live in the then or the now?

They silenced their phone and went to the peephole. Outside, Birdie was pacing their stoop. Van opened the door.

"Any news?" they asked as Birdie bolted inside.

Gem had gone with Birdie yesterday to the camp director's house to deliver Birdie's newsletter. Van knew, from their audition at the Youth Orchestra in Dublin, that waiting to hear on something you wanted was brutal.

"People who say no news is good news are full of it," Birdie said. "So, what do you need our hands for? My grandma's visiting from Oklahoma, so I can only stay a few minutes. Technically, I'm not supposed to be here."

Van gestured at their mam's behemoth sewing machine in the corner of the living room. "We're going to make Gem's costume."

Birdie looked confused, so Van added: "For her solo at the recital? To replace the bad costume? So she can still perform . . . you know, since she quit because of the . . . bra thing?"

"Oh yeah," Birdie said, too quickly. "Right."

Had Gem not told Birdie the real reason she quit dance? There'd been nothing Van couldn't tell Caro . . . at least, before they'd moved. Since the move, things were different. FaceTime was awkward, especially with filters, and their text threads were mostly just GIFs. But before Van could make sense of Gem keeping this secret from Birdie, their front door swung open, and Marley and Gem bounded in.

"We checked on Phoebe before we left," Marley said.

"And?" Birdie asked.

"The same," Gem said, looking down. "She was calling for Artemis in her sleep. She sounded so tortured . . ." Gem's face twisted with such pain that Van came close to offering her a hug. Instead they reminded Gem:

"We're doing this today to help her. Your costume, your wish. If we grant it, it might get Phoebe home in time."

Van set out the tea, a full squeezy-bear of honey, and the biscuits. They brought out their materials—the pattern they'd downloaded, the bolt of black fabric from Mam's closet. They pulled up a bookmarked page on their laptop and faced the screen toward the others.

"Gem, meet your new costume," they said, nerves fluttering in their chest. "What do you think?"

"Like the one from the TikTok video," Gem said, bright-eyed.

"You said you liked it."

"You can really make this?"

"We really can," Van said.

"I can dance in that," Gem whispered. "I can get onstage in that."

"Then let's get started," Van said, "because Birdie can't stay long—"

"No, I can stay," Birdie said, and crossed her arms over her chest. "Long as it takes."

"I thought your grandma—"

"I was wrong," Birdie lied. "That was cancelled." She was over at the sewing machine, pushing all the wrong buttons. "How does this thing work?"

Van redirected Birdie, putting her on cloth cutting, stationing themself before the sewing machine, and handing Gem and Marley a pair of hot-glue guns to add a silver fringe. Van worked the machine as Mam had taught them. For a few minutes, everyone was quiet.

"So you're back on the dance team now?" Birdie said.

"Not exactly," Gem said. "But if this costume comes together, I'm going to ask Coach if I can perform in the recital next weekend. Like you said, Phoebe needs us."

"It's going to work out," Marley said. "And so is Birdie's newsletter."

Van noticed Birdie look to Gem then, as if wanting her to agree, but Gem was busy hot-gluing, so Birdie sighed and went back to cutting.

"That newsletter would convince me to give you a scholarship, Birdie," Van decided to say. "You made Camp Evergreen sound brilliant."

"You should come this summer, Van," Gem said.

"I wish," Van said, reinforcing a seam. "My da's taking me to Hawaii."

"Lucky," Marley said.

"You haven't met my da's girlfriend," Van said. "All I really want is to go back to Ireland over break, but Mam can't afford it."

"Wait," Birdie said, "is that your wish?"

Van swallowed. "I hope not. No one's giving out scholarships for me to go home." They paused, feeling Birdie's eyes on them. "It's not an arrow. It's a dart, actually. You know the game? My friend Caro and I used to play it in their da's pub."

"So your wish is about Caro?" Birdie asked.

"Dunno," Van said a little irritably. They didn't share

the news that Caro had finally called Van back. It was easier to focus on the others' wishes than it was to face their own. Van's wishes had a history of not coming true.

Maybe Gem's wish or Birdie's wish would be enough to fix Phoebe, and she could get home, and Van would never have to fail.

They put their head down and sewed.

TWENTY-FOUR

Birdie

Good, you're all here," Birdie said as she ducked inside the crabapples Friday morning before school.

"Your text did say *Emergency Meeting*," Gem said. She was wearing a new dress, white with blue flowers and shiny buttons down the front. She'd done something different to her hair. Birdie couldn't tell exactly what. Meanwhile, Birdie was in cutoffs and some dumb T-shirt her dad had gotten for free at a conference. Her hair sucked in its boring ponytail. She hadn't even thought about cleaning up for the last day of school, but now she wished she had.

At the base of the crabapple tree, the fairy lay sleeping. Every day she looked weaker, and last night Birdie had tossed in bed, wishing their efforts would make her better—until she realized there was no one up there catching her wishes anymore.

Her heart pounded as she laid her letter on the ground. "Someone open it for me. I can't."

Marley tore it open. His eyes flicked back and forth as he read. "You did it! Birdie, you got a scholarship!"

"Get out of town!" Birdie fell back in the dirt with relief. "I'm going to camp, y'all. I can go." The words didn't seem real, but they were. She'd done it. She read the letter for herself.

"Congratulations," Gem said, and hugged her sideways. It felt so good that Birdie closed her eyes. Hot tears slipped down her cheeks. She'd done something she thought was impossible. She'd made her own magic.

As she held the letter, everything suddenly felt within reach. Phoebe flying home in time to save Artemis. Birdie and Gem having an unforgettable summer at camp.

"Wake up, Phoebe," Van said gently. "Birdie made her wish come true."

The fairy blinked and turned toward Birdie, slowly struggling to her feet.

"There's a letter and everything," Birdie whispered. "Proof."

"You wished very hard on this," Phoebe said.

Birdie nodded. "I did."

"Now I can show you the ritual," Phoebe said. "What happens when wishes come true."

Birdie met Van's eyes, then Marley's, then Gem's. All were twinkling, but none so much as Birdie's.

"Do you still have your charm?" Phoebe asked.

Birdie slid the gold chain down her wrist. She felt it give as it passed over her palm. She put the pine-tree charm in Phoebe's hand and watched the fairy's fingers close around it.

"Stay still." Phoebe closed her eyes. Birdie closed hers, too, but had to peek. She saw the fairy reaching toward her but not near enough to touch. It felt like a long while passed. Birdie tried thinking about camp, because maybe it would help if she were in the zone. She tried to see herself diving into some lake with Gem. Sunlight on the water. Sunscreen in her eyes. And then—

It felt like the first half-second when you leap off a high swing. When you're still going up, before you remember gravity. Birdie knew her feet were on the ground, but it felt like she was flying. Through her squint, she saw a golden halo of light rise out of her chest.

"Oh. Wow," someone said. Maybe Van. Birdie couldn't see the others for the light coming out of her. Shining through her.

It was the prettiest thing she'd ever seen. It was *her*. She was so pretty, on the inside. Where it mattered. Birdie never would have guessed.

"What is that?" Gem whispered.

"It's called a Granting," Phoebe said, summoning the halo of light nearer. "It's what Birdie made come true. Now all there is to do is join the Granting with her wish."

"And then you won't be gray anymore?" Birdie heard Marley ask.

She saw Phoebe smile through the golden glow. "That's the plan."

Phoebe never touched the Granting. It hovered above the fairy's fingers, responding to her gestures, moving nearer the pine charm in her other hand.

"This is my favorite part," Phoebe said. She drew the wish and Granting nearer. Then they touched, and Birdie held her breath as charm and orb . . . bounced off each other. It reminded Birdie of magnets with like poles. What was the word?

Repel.

"Strange," Phoebe said, her brow furrowing. She brought the Granting near the wish again. Again, it bounced away from Birdie's pine-tree charm.

"What's wrong?" Birdie asked. "What should I do?"

Phoebe trembled, seeming to force the orb of light toward the charm. But it was like there was an invisible wall between the two. The more Phoebe tried, the farther Birdie's Granting backed away.

Now Phoebe took the charm in her hand and whisked

it near the Granting. But the Granting zipped backward, high through the boughs of the crabapples. Birdie looked up in horror to see it nosedive straight down. Toward her. She screamed as it slammed into her chest.

"Birdie!"

The next thing Birdie knew, Gem was helping her up off the ground. "What happened? Where'd it go?" She felt like the wind had been knocked out of her.

Gem shook her head. She was still holding Birdie's hand.

"Maybe it's too late," Van said. "Maybe Phoebe's too sick."

"No," the fairy said, looking at Birdie. "Something's missing. From your wish."

Birdie felt Gem's hand drop away. And it killed her, that feeling. Then it filled her . . . with rage. She spun on Gem and pointed her finger. "You."

"Me?"

"If there's something missing from my wish, it's because—"

"I dare you, Birdie," Gem said. Her eyes narrowed and her stare turned cold. A bolt of lightning cracked the sky as she said, "I just dare you to blame your broken wish on me."

TWENTY-FIVE

Gem

Gem was back on the therapist's couch.

She'd been doing so much better—even her parents could see it. When she'd told them her plan to dance in the recital, the whole family had gone out for ice cream. Everyone seemed too happy, like Gem had been elected president. She told them they were being extra, but when she practiced her solo in the costume that Van designed, Gem got goose bumps from how good it felt.

Then Birdie's wish had failed, and it sent Gem down again.

She hated seeing Phoebe's face when Birdie's Granting didn't work. Gem blamed Birdie; she couldn't help it.

It wasn't like Birdie didn't know how much was at stake. And then Birdie turned it around and tried to blame Gem! What was wrong with her?

Last night, lying in bed, Gem got scared that her own wish granting might not be as simple as dancing in the recital.

Birdie's wish had shown them all they were in over their heads. They could turn to no one for help. Phoebe was dying. And now, on top of everything else, Gem had to sit on this couch and stare at a fish tank, and pretend she was just your-average-anxious to the old guy in the sweater vest her parents had hired as her therapist.

"How do you feel when you imagine yourself dancing alone on a stage?" he was saying when Gem saw something flash through the window past his head.

She blinked and there it was again. Her brother's hand. Waving. Pointing. Toward the door. Marley was too short to clear the window, but she saw his Transformers watch.

When her dad dropped her off at this appointment, the plan was for Marley to join her parents on some important carpet-shopping errand. He must have gotten out of it. But why had he come here? Gem's stomach seized with nerves.

"I need to use the bathroom," she said.

The therapist pointed at the door. Gem bolted for it and found Marley in the lobby, looking panicked.

"What are you doing here?"

"You have to come," he said urgently.

"Come where? What's wrong?"

"It's Phoebe." He glanced in the direction of the thera-pist's office, reading Gem's mind. "Make up an excuse."

Gem shook her head. If something bad happened to Phoebe, Gem didn't want to waste another moment.

"Let's just go," she said. "By the time he thinks to come look for me, we'll be gone."

A moment later, they were out the door—Gem on foot, racing Marley on his bike, back to their neighbor-hood, back to the crabapples. As they ducked inside the boughs, Gem prepared herself for the worst. If Phoebe was dead—

To see it was worse than to imagine it. The fairy was no longer curled cocoonlike at the base of the tree. She lay flat on her back, gold eyes open, arms slack at her sides. Her chest was still.

Gem looked at Marley. His eyes shone with tears.

"I came out to check on her, and—" He let out a sob. "You took CPR. Do you still remember it?"

Gem fell on her knees before the fairy, her mind clear-ing of everything but the steps she'd learned at the YMCA on that awkward mannequin. How many breaths and how many compressions? How far back did she tip the chin?

What if she broke the fairy's ribs? Would this even work on a magical creature? Gem barely knew how it worked on humans.

"What should I do?" Marley asked.

Hearing her brother's voice made Gem feel calmer. She was used to giving him orders.

"Go inside. Bring water and a pillow. Your phone."

Gem's phone was still on the therapist's couch. But who would she even call? 911? Birdie and Van? Her mom? She wanted to cry, but she wouldn't. She pressed two fingers to the fairy's neck, where she thought the pulse should be. Nothing.

"Phoebe," she said, leaning close. "Hold on. Please." She placed her hands over the fairy's chest. Had Gem ever had to do something so important before? She felt too big and too clumsy, but she pressed firmly, then waited for the fairy's chest to rise. She did it thirty times.

Gem thought of the first time she'd seen Phoebe, that feeling of lightness within her. She thought of the fairy's weight in her backpack all through school, how proud Gem had felt to be responsible for her.

"Please." Her voice broke. "Phoebe, we need you."

She pressed her mouth around the fairy's, and she breathed. Once, twice.

Pulse—nothing.

Gem did more compressions. She thought of Birdie's wish, how painful it had been when the granting didn't work. Why hadn't they realized that, in Phoebe's state, the effort to grant might kill her?

Another breath. Another. The ground stirred beneath her. Was it working?

"Groovy! No!" Marley crashed back into the crabapples. A second later, Gem felt the unmistakable thunder of their giant dog hurtling straight at her.

"I must have left the front door open!" Marley cried.

Groovy bounded at Gem. She tried to shield the fairy, but the Great Dane's tail was up. There would be no throwing the 120-pound beast off her scent.

"Groovy!" Gem screamed, yanking at his collar, but even with all of her strength, she couldn't stop him. He skidded to a halt before the fairy and—

Delivered a slobbery kiss the full length of Phoebe's face. He whined playfully, confused. And then Gem heard . . . was that a fairy giggle?

"Help me get him off," Gem told Marley, who gripped onto Groovy's collar too.

At last they wrenched the dog away, commanding him to lie down.

"Phoebe?" Gem said. "We're *so* sorry . . ."

The fairy's eyes blinked open. A smile crept onto her

face, and she stretched her arms over her head luxuriously. "It's been so long since I've felt the refreshment of a star shower on my skin. I needed that."

Gem looked at Marley. Neither of them could seem to decide whether to laugh or cry.

"Don't be rude! Introduce me to your friend!" Phoebe said, pointing at Groovy.

And so they did. The dog couldn't stop covering Phoebe with kisses, but Phoebe couldn't get enough of them. She laughed as strands of drool darkened her dress. She climbed atop the Great Dane's head, nestled her face in his giant ear, and sighed contentedly.

Marley taught Phoebe how to play fetch. Throwing twigs for the dog was the most active Phoebe had been since she came down with the Grays. For the first time since Birdie's wish failed, Gem wasn't despondent. Part of her felt guilty that Van and Birdie weren't here to experience this, but also, it was nice just to be with her brother.

"I knew you'd save her," Marley said.

"I didn't," Gem said. Was it the CPR or Groovy that had brought the fairy back to life? Gem didn't care, so long as Phoebe stayed this way.

When she looked at Marley, she was startled to see that he looked older, his face a little less chubby, his feet suddenly huge. Her little brother had graduated elementary school. Next year they'd both be on the middle school campus. It was hard for Gem to believe.

"Marley?" Gem said. "What was your wish?"

Marley pulled at some grass. Finally, head low, he said, "I wished for Felix Howard to contract a flesh-eating bacteria."

"You did not." Gem laughed until she realized Marley was serious.

"It's called necrotizing fasciitis. If you image-search it online, you won't be able to unsee it. But if anyone deserves—"

"Hold on . . ." Gem turned to Phoebe, who was watching their conversation from atop Groovy's sleeping head. "You said it was a good wish, Phoebe. You almost *granted* it. If you hadn't eaten it, would Felix Howard have actually . . ."

Felix made Gem's blood boil, but she didn't wish him physical harm. She wouldn't have thought Marley did either. Or that Phoebe would use her powers like that.

"I was granting the *true wish* at its core," Phoebe said. "A wish of protection."

"But—"

"There are the *words* of any wish," Phoebe said, giving Gem a pointed look. "And then there is the truth beneath them."

"So Birdie's wish," Gem said, "to go to camp . . ."

Phoebe nodded. "There is something underneath."

"Why didn't you tell us that?" Gem said. "Your life is at stake! And if she'd known, maybe Birdie could have made the other part come true—"

"I didn't need to tell you. You already know," Phoebe said, fluffing one of Groovy's ears like a pillow. "Is your wish *only* to get a trophy?"

Gem was quiet. She knew the trophy was an emblem. It was worth probably $1.75, but it represented something far more valuable. The thing was, Gem had wished for it *because* what it represented was impossible. It involved going back in time to the body she'd had last year, to the confidence she'd had last year.

But then Van had opened a back door into Gem's wish. One that she hadn't known was there. So, her wish changed. It became a wish to dance on her own terms. Without thinking about her body. Without feeling like she'd been stuffed inside a boob-shaped suit. Without obsessing over all the eyes on her.

Even if her wish only lasted the length of her favorite song, if Gem could get onstage and feel *free*, she would know that at least it was possible to fit in her skin again. It would give her hope for the future.

So, okay. Birdie's wish was missing something. Did Birdie know what it was? If Gem tried to go over there and tell Birdie what Phoebe had told them today, would Birdie even want to hear it? Or would it turn into another fight where Birdie thought Gem was criticizing her?

Of course it would.

Fine, then. Birdie was on her own. Gem had enough to worry about with her wish. The recital—and their deadline to heal Phoebe's wings—was in four days, and her costume wasn't enough. Gem had work to do.

TWENTY-SIX

Van

Van slipped into the crabapples alone on Friday morning. They glanced toward Gem's house, and then, with shaking hands, lifted the sleeping fairy in their arms.

They were just about to tuck Phoebe inside a teddy bear–shaped backpack when the fairy's eyes shot open.

Both of them yelped, but Phoebe's yelp had no glamour, and the sound rattled Van to their core. They ducked their head between their shoulders and almost dropped the bag.

"You're awake," they said. "I was just, er, how are you?"

"Low." Phoebe wore a tortured look. "I miss home. My Wishwell. I am weak and worried about Artemis. I should not have come to Texas."

"I have an idea," Van said. "Something that may help. Would you like to go on an adventure?"

The fairy tilted her head, intrigued. "Will there be snacks?"

Van pulled a fruit leather from the backpack, then left a note at the base of the crabapple trunk:

> B, G, and M,
> I've taken Phoebe with me to Dallas. Sorry I didn't
> explain sooner, but I hope you'll understand. I had to.
> It's part of my wishwork. We'll be safe—and home in
> time for Gem's recital.
> Van

"Needs honey!" Phoebe rated the fruit leather as Van dashed out from the crabapples, teddy bear backpack slung over their shoulder.

Da had given them the backpack for Christmas. They were too old for it—you couldn't pay them to bring it to school—but the stuffy factor would give Van cover tonight if they wanted to sleep with it at the hotel.

"Mam's waiting in the car," Van explained to Phoebe. "She's a grown-up, so . . . you know the drill."

Luckily, Mam asked no questions when Van dashed out from the crabapples to her idling car. She was focused on which freeway exit she'd have to take to reach their downtown hotel, and on making sure, for the eighteenth time, that she'd put the symphony tickets in her purse.

The drive lulled Phoebe to sleep. It wasn't five minutes before Van heard her tiny snores inside the bear bag. They turned up the radio a touch so Mam wouldn't catch on.

It hadn't crossed Van's mind to take Phoebe to Dallas—until Birdie's wish failed. Van had been relying on Birdie and Gem making their wishes come true first, so that Van might watch and learn. After all, the girls at least knew what their wishes *were*. But when that orb of light went back inside Birdie, Van knew they had to step up their game. They had two days and one night to heal the fairy.

Fairies loved music, and playing music professionally *was* a wish of Van's. Maybe something would happen tonight that would get Van closer to that goal. Maybe they'd bump into the flautist in the philharmonic bathroom. If Phoebe's life depended on it, Van could strike up a conversation with a grown-up idol. Maybe.

They'd started playing the flute in Caro's da's pub, where they'd also learned to play darts. It wasn't an impossible connection. A flute charm would have been too on the nose. It wasn't like Birdie's charm was a golden letter granting her a scholarship. But then, Birdie's wish was *missing* something. *What?* Van felt sorry for her—and anxious to know how to make sure their own wish was complete.

"I said, your head's in the clouds today, Van," their

mam said, clearly for the second time. She merged onto the highway, their tiny red VW falling between huge white SUVs.

Van looked automatically toward the clouds, but there weren't any. Or else there was nothing but clouds. The whole sky was flat and gray. The road was flat and gray. They reminded themself they had a sleeping fairy on their lap, and that, somewhere out there, beyond this stretch of gray, was a big city they'd never been to, with music for them both.

They tried thinking about the symphony, and not what Gem or Marley or Birdie would do when they came to the crabapples and found the note. Van hadn't asked because they didn't want permission, because if anyone said no, they still would have taken Phoebe. But they didn't like imagining the others mad. It was easy to picture a fight erupting between Gem and Birdie, all because Van had taken Phoebe.

"You're still looking forward to tonight?" Mam said.

"Of course."

"It's been ages since I've seen *Peter Pan*," Mam said. "And this original version will be more your speed than the Disney film."

Van had never seen *Peter Pan*—Disney or original—but they were familiar with the characters. When they were little, their da had given them a Tinker Bell toothbrush, and they remembered scraping the graphic off with their fingernail because the prim and pretty fairy made them sad. Real fairies were far lovelier in their misshapen ways.

"You sure you're all right?" Mam asked.

"It's just," Van said, stalling, "some trouble with friends."

Mam turned down the radio. "Go on."

"Well, there's one friend who's always saying things like *You don't understand me*, and this other friend who's always saying things like *It's your fault I don't understand*. And they're both really angry. And they're both maybe right."

"These turbulent years," their mam said. "Everyone growing up at their own speed. It's not a race, though it can feel like one." She tapped her fingers on the steering wheel. "You know I didn't menstruate until I was near fourteen—"

"Mam!" Van clutched their face. "I don't want to know that! You were doing so well before."

"Was I, now?" she asked, sounding proud.

"Can we keep things general, please?"

"I'll be as vague as possible."

Mercifully, Van had yet to enter puberty in any noticeable way, but they had been to an endocrinologist to discuss puberty blockers. The sessions were mortifying, but Van knew that when the time came, they'd be grateful for the option. And Mam's support.

"Speaking generally," Mam said, "I understand it's hard to feel you're being left behind."

Van nodded—that was Birdie.

"But it's equally hard to feel you're hurtling forward, into the unknown—alone."

Gem.

When you put it that way, it made sense. Gem and Birdie might be in the same room, but when it came to how they felt inside, they were as far away as Texas and the North Star.

"As much as you want a friend to reach their hand back to you, Van, you must make sure you have your own hand extended forward too," Mam said, and Van realized, yet again, that their mam assumed they were talking about themself, not two other human beings.

"Jesus, Mary, and Joseph, I've gone so vague I've missed our exit!" Mam threw on her blinker and boldly crossed three lanes of traffic as the Dallas skyline came brightly into view.

In the concert hall, Van wore their good sweater and their nicest pair of pants. They squeezed Mam's hand and sat on the edge of their seat. As the musicians tuned their instruments, Van held their backpack on their lap and looked around.

Sand-colored columns framed a maroon-curtained stage. A black chandelier hung from the ceiling. Mam had splurged on seats in the front row of the balcony, but what

Van longed for most was a seat in the flute section of the orchestra pit. Someday.

When the conductor walked out, and the audience stilled, and the first notes filled the concert hall, Van got goose bumps. The music was a cold drink of water when you were very thirsty. Van hadn't realized how thirsty they were. The flutes were abundant. The overture pulsed with a beautiful ache that felt familiar. Van held the bear bag at an angle so that Phoebe could see and hear through a small gap in the zipper.

When Peter Pan introduced Tinker Bell onstage, Van waited to see a version of the feminine fairy from their old toothbrush. To their surprise, the fairy in this performance was depicted by a simple flash of light. It flitted around the auditorium in time with the flutes.

Van felt Phoebe stir. They leaned subtly forward, making sure Mam wasn't looking.

"What do you think?" they whispered.

"What is this spectacle?" Phoebe coughed.

Van slipped her the program, smiling. It was right they had brought Phoebe here, even if it broke the crabapple pact. This performance was all about childhood—how wild and epic, how eternal, it was. It poked fun at adults. Van was surprised how much Mam laughed at those parts. When they looked over at her—smiling, shining—they saw the girl in their mother. Mam wore an adult over her true kid's body, like a coat. Van knew that coat would eventually drop onto them, like it dropped onto everyone, but for now they wiggled their shoulders and enjoyed the sense of lightness.

After intermission, the tone of the performance shifted from playful to grave: Tinker Bell had been poisoned. She was dying. The music ceased. Van held their breath as Peter Pan walked to the edge of the stage. When he addressed the audience, he seemed to be looking right at Van. He told them there was only one way to save Tinker Bell.

"Do you believe in fairies?" he asked. "If you believe, clap your hands!"

Van and Mam looked at each other. Laughing, they joined the rest of the audience and began to clap. In an instant—Van didn't know how it happened—both of them were crying. They leaned against Mam, held fast to Phoebe in the bag, and felt grateful. To believe was a wondrous thing.

At the end of the performance, everyone rose to applaud. Van whistled, bouncing on their heels as the orchestra took bows. When the curtain dropped and they lifted the backpack off their seat, it weighed less than it should have. They peeked inside. And found only a shredded program.

No.

Van's heart seized. They checked the bag again, every

zipped pocket, but the fairy was gone. Had she *died*? Had the Grays come for her at last? Was this what happened to a fairy at the end of her life? Or had Van's carelessness caused this? Their eyes pricked with anxious tears as they scanned the floor. The aisles. The hundreds of unassuming people milling around the audience, trying to get home.

What had Van done?

"Can I go have a look at the orchestra pit?" they asked Mam, trying to hide their panic.

"Sure. I'll meet you in the lobby," Mam said, and gave their forehead a kiss.

Van pushed against the current of people trying to leave the hall. They headed down the stairs, up the center aisle, and eventually found themself before the stage. They were so afraid they felt faint. If anything happened to Phoebe, Van would never forgive themself.

But then, just when they had nearly given up hope, they saw the unmistakable form of the fairy climbing the stairs stage left. She was gray and fragile, her wings a fright, but she was still here. She was okay.

"Phoebe!" They raced toward her, swooping her up in their arms and nestling her back in the bag. "You scared me!"

"I wanted to meet her," Phoebe said, her eyes holding sorrow and hope. "Tinker Bell."

How could Van scold her for that? Though their heart

was still racing, they understood. Sometimes you wanted to meet a kindred spirit so badly, it didn't matter whether they were real or not. It didn't matter what you had to risk to find them.

Van zipped Phoebe up and gave her a hug through the backpack, thinking of Birdie and Gem and Marley as they headed back to Mam.

That night they curled on their side in the big white hotel bed. Mam had a glass of wine at dinner and fell asleep right away. Van unzipped the bear bag and snuggled close to Phoebe. The fairy's breath came slow. Van thought about the music, how, during the *allegro*, the flute and the oboe sometimes tangled, sometimes journeyed parallel. They thought about Mam's words earlier, about hands reaching forward and back. They thought about saving Tinker Bell, and losing Phoebe, and finding her again. They thought about what Birdie's wish was missing, and whether Gem's would come true at the recital. They thought about their own wish. They thought about the *adagio*, that slow bridge in the performance, connecting the quicker movements.

Then they sat up in bed in the dark Dallas hotel, and they knew what they had to do.

TWENTY-SEVEN

Birdie

G et dressed," Van said when Birdie opened her front door Saturday morning. "The recital's in an hour."

"No thanks," Birdie said, crossing her arms over her chest. She was wearing pretty embarrassing old Moana pajamas and trying not to care. "She doesn't want me there."

"Birdie. You've never missed one of Gem's dance recitals. Eight years in a row. You're going to wreck your streak."

"Yeah, well, things change. Streaks end."

Birdie moved to close the door on Van. She was mad at the kid for taking Phoebe out of the crabapples without telling any of them. For one thing, it went against the rules they'd all agreed on. For another, if Van hadn't taken Phoebe to Dallas, then Birdie and Gem wouldn't have gotten into a huge fight yesterday about what was best for the fairy.

Van put their hand out and stopped the door from closing. "I skipped room service for this. You're coming."

"Huh?"

"My mam and I, we stayed at this fancy hotel, and we'd been talking about the room service breakfast for months—I was going to get the pancakes, she was going to . . . anyway—in the middle of the night, I figured it out! I made Mam leave at six a.m. to get back. Because I had a feeling I'd need to drag you to this recital."

"You figured *what* out?" Birdie said.

"My wish. It's not to go back to Ireland and play darts in the pub with Caro. It's to have friends *here*. Friends as good as Caro was. Friends, plural. And you and Gem are my best hope, so." Van unzipped this weird stuffed bear–shaped backpack and offered Birdie a peek at Phoebe inside.

"Please Birdie?" Phoebe said.

The fairy looked so cute and so frail, Birdie couldn't stand it. She didn't feel like saying "Okay" yet, but she didn't slam the door either. She opened it a couple of inches wider. Van took the hint and came inside.

Birdie's mom was in the kitchen, frowning at her laptop, probably paying bills. Birdie led Van down the hallway to her room. Van looked at the stuff tacked up on Birdie's walls—a calendar from her grandma featuring exotic birds, some sketches and plans for new comics, a lot of pictures and souvenir stuff from things she'd done with Gem. Birdie was so used to her walls she barely saw them anymore, but Van's eyes were wide, like Birdie had thumbtacked up the *Mona Lisa* instead of old receipts from Baskin-Robbins.

Birdie crouched down next to Phoebe, who was still inside the bag. She let herself feel how much she'd missed the fairy yesterday. It felt like someone was pouring something warm down her insides, and she didn't know if it was a good feeling or not.

"Did she like the performance?" Birdie asked.

Van sat down beside her, put their hand on Phoebe's wing. "We both did. I think she'll like the recital, too. What are you going to wear?"

"Who cares?" Birdie said, tugging at her old pajamas. She half wanted to wear them just to show how little she cared.

"I care," Van said, which surprised Birdie. She didn't think of Van as interested in clothes. At least not like the girls at school who cared about them, who all wore versions of the same exact thing.

"This could be a big day," Van said. "You'll want to feel comfortable. Trust me."

Birdie's mom usually made her wear some terrible dress and scratchy tights to Gem's recitals. She'd gone through eight of them itching like she was at church. She liked Van's reasoning better, and so she chose a yellow T-shirt with an owl on the front and a pair of black leggings she thought almost made her look cool.

Van turned away, looking at Birdie's sketches, giving her privacy to change.

"Okay, I'm ready," Birdie said, tugging on her shoes.

"Perfect," Van said as Birdie looked in the mirror on the door of her closet, licking her finger to smooth down the cowlick.

"Van?" She met the kid's eyes in the mirror. "I feel like a failure."

"You're *not* a failure, Birdie."

Van put their hands on Birdie's shoulders, and Birdie didn't know why, but she got the urge to close her eyes. It wasn't because it was awkward; it was because it felt so nice.

"Your wish is—" Van said.

"Missing something—" Birdie's voice broke.

"*In progress.* So don't quit on it yet."

Birdie nodded. She liked this side of Van. She hefted the backpack with Phoebe onto her shoulder, and the two them started toward the front door.

"Mom, we're going to Gem's recital."

"I thought she quit," her mother called from the kitchen. Birdie waited but didn't hear the scrape of the metal chair, the signal her mom was coming to have more of a conversation.

"It's complicated," she called back. "I'll be home after."

"I hope you're wearing tights!" her mom shouted as Birdie rolled her eyes at Van and closed the door.

"I googled the fastest way to the auditorium," Van said as they grabbed their bikes. They pointed down the street.

"Uh-uh." Birdie shook her head.

"Now what's wrong?" Van asked.

"We can't show up without flowers." Birdie turned her bike in the opposite direction. "Come on, I know a spot."

The hall was dark by the time Birdie and Van slipped into the audience, each holding wildflower bouquets. In the glow of the stage light, Birdie saw Marley's head bobbing in one of the front rows, next to Mr. and Mrs. Cash.

Birdie always sat with them. This year, no one had even mentioned coming to pick her up in their car. And for a moment, Birdie felt angry about this—shouldn't Gem's parents care about her, even a little? But then she noticed something that made her heart swell. Right next to Marley, there were two empty seats. She tugged on Van's shirt as they sidestepped people down the rows. They claimed their seats just as the curtain came up.

Marley turned and grinned at them. *You made it,* he mouthed. His eyes shot to the backpack, and Birdie knew what he was asking. She nodded, gave him a quick peek inside.

Mrs. Cash reached across Marley to squeeze Birdie's hand. "Thanks for being here." She looked at Van and nodded, smiling. "Both of you."

For a while, it was the usual recital, and Birdie felt her usual way. Excited at first, then a little bored, then amused by the tiniest kids who tripped over their costumes and had no clue what was going on. There were the usual moms crowding the front, holding up their phones to video their kids. There were screaming babies in the audience, so much red lipstick, and problems with the spotlight.

And then, just as Birdie was about to excuse herself to go to the bathroom, came the opening notes of Gem's solo. The stage was dark. Then filled with light. And there she was at the center, curled in a tuck position on the floor. Birdie's best friend, in her starting pose.

Birdie knew the dance. Not like she could do it or anything, but she knew that in a few more seconds, Gem would rise and spread her arms, and shine bright as the sun. Birdie wanted this success for Gem so badly she had tears in her eyes.

Here was a true wish. It was undeniable.

Birdie sat still and waited.

TWENTY-EIGHT

Gem

Gem's solo culminated in a triple pirouette that she landed in a split as the song hit its final note. When the lights went out, she lay there for a moment, out of breath, face resting on her shin, and thought: *Remember this feeling.*

She'd done the thing she thought she could never do again. She'd danced, in front of people—and not felt shame, but *glory.* Her body hadn't been the point. An energy inside her had shone through. She knew this was just a moment, that in a second, she'd stand up and walk offstage, and life would go on in its sometimes pleasant, sometimes painful, often boring way. But this? She'd needed this. And she'd made it happen. She wasn't going to forget it.

Backstage was the usual flutter, people hugging her and pushing past her and getting lipstick on her sleeves. Gem smiled and heard her voice say, "Thanks, you too," but she felt outside herself for the last two numbers before curtain call.

When she walked back onstage with the rest of the team to bow, Gem stared hard through the stage lights at the audience, like she hadn't done since her very first recital when she was three years old and needing to see her mom's face. This time it was Birdie she was looking for, though she didn't realize it until she saw her best friend's eyes.

Wet with tears. Birdie never cried.

It made Gem's own eyes sting, and she waved, even though they weren't supposed to.

"Gemima Cash has earned this year's Golden Rose," Coach's voice said over the PA.

Gem put her hands out, and there it was, hefty in its marble base, gleaming under the spotlight. Her parents cheered. Marley whistled. Gem noticed Van next to Birdie, which meant Phoebe was here.

The fairy was in the audience. She had been here when Gem made her wish come true.

Gem never would have danced today if not for Phoebe. She thought she'd outgrown the Golden Rose wish, but the fairy had been right: Gem's wish had grown with her.

But would it help Phoebe? Would it heal her? Was it enough?

"You were brilliant," Marley said when he found Gem backstage. He came with Birdie, Van, and this teddy bear–shaped backpack that could only contain one thing. "Mom and Dad are waiting outside—"

Gem grabbed her brother's hand and beckoned the others to follow her into the captains' dressing room. It was a space reserved for select eighth graders, but every-one knew they were outside doing a balloon ceremony and pictures for at least the next five minutes.

Gem locked the door. There were jazz shoes every-where and flowers propped against the mirrors. It smelled like baby powder and slightly sweaty feet.

"Phoebe?" she said.

Birdie unzipped the backpack. From inside, the fairy held up her frail, gray head.

"Do you have the charm?" Phoebe whispered.

Gem nodded. Shook her wrist to send the chain slid-ing down her arm and out of the black sleeve Van had hemmed.

"Let's do this," Phoebe said.

Gem reached for Birdie's hand and squeezed. "Does it hurt?"

Birdie swallowed, then squeezed back. "No."

Gem had gotten used to thinking of Phoebe as sick, as weak, but when the fairy set her mind to Gem's wish, Gem felt the most powerful tranquility. She stood still and watched the fairy close her eyes and focus. It was like being on a boat at sunset, where nothing was expected of you other than to experience beauty and peace.

Soft light everywhere. Warmth and a shimmery quiet. A pleasant tingle rippled through Gem, and then she saw it—the golden orb of light passing out of her body and into the air. It hovered in front of Phoebe like an angel's halo.

Everything simply felt . . . right. The chain slipped off Gem's wrist, gravitating toward the orb, and then, with a bright pulse, Gem saw her entire wish flash before her eyes—

She saw herself at three years old, holding her mother's leg as she stepped into the dance studio for the first time. She saw herself at four and six and nine and ten, doing a thousand pliés at the barre. She saw herself pirouetting in gas stations, off diving boards, and in her cabin at camp. She saw her face when Coach put up the picture of her solo costume, how she'd come close to throwing up. Then at the dinner table, fighting with her parents, insisting she had quit. She saw herself in the crabapples, doing the Crank with Phoebe and Van and Birdie. She saw herself before her bedroom mirror, trying on the new costume her friends had sewn for her. She saw the Golden Rose trophy, which was so much more than a trophy, being placed into her hands.

And then Gem was back in the dressing room with Phoebe and the others. The light from the orb blasted outward. Gem watched it join with her golden charm and make new light that grew brighter, hotter. She felt it wash over her, into her.

When she blinked, the room looked normal again, but something was different. Gem was different. Her wish was granted. She'd granted it. And—

"Phoebe!" Birdie said, eyes wide and pointing at the fairy. "You're . . ."

Color had returned to Phoebe's cheeks and lips, to her eyes and skin, to her astonishingly beautiful dress and hat.

"Thank you, Gem," the fairy said in a clearer voice than she'd used a moment ago. Phoebe was radiating such beauty and magic that Gem could have exploded with pride.

Healed. The fairy was—

No. When the fairy turned, Gem saw Phoebe's wings were still brittle and gray. She tried to spread them, then winced in pain. She tucked them away, chagrin in her eyes. She looked up at the drop-panel ceiling of the dressing room, as if toward the North Star. And Gem saw in her eyes how far away, how impossible, going home still was.

"Come," the fairy said. "Let's go back to the crabapples. We have more work to do."

TWENTY-NINE

Birdie

Who's up for some celebratory ice cream?" Gem's dad asked when they met in the parking lot after Gem had changed.

Birdie loved going for ice cream with the Cashes. They let you order anything you wanted, even a banana split. On an ordinary day, Birdie's heaven was forking a banana doused in fudgy, melty whipped cream, those little nuts . . . but this was no ordinary day.

Phoebe was halfway healed, and they could take no chances getting busted now by Gem's parents or some teenager scooping ice cream at Baskin-Robbins. They needed to keep the fairy in the bear bag until they were safe at the crabapples.

And then they needed Van to step up with their wish, since Birdie's had already proven hopeless. Maybe Van's wish would be enough to fix Phoebe the rest of the way.

"How do we lose your folks, Gem?" Van asked out of the side of their mouth.

Gem didn't answer, so Birdie improvised. "Sorry, Mr. and Mrs. Cash, but I kinda had something planned to celebrate Gem's amazing performance today. Just kids." She put her hand on Marley's shoulder so he'd know he was included. "Can we raincheck on the ice cream?"

"Sure," Mr. Cash said with a kind of frowny smile. "You kids go have fun."

"Way to go, Birdie," Marley said under his breath as Birdie and Van grabbed their bikes.

It was a mile back to the crabapples, and the pavement was cooking the soles of Birdie's shoes. She unzipped a bit more of the backpack, trying to give Phoebe some air. Inside, the fairy was restless. Birdie couldn't imagine being stuck between dying and fixed, with your only hope being four kids who didn't know what the heck they were doing.

"You could teach a class on getting rid of parents." Van walked their bike next to Birdie.

"Yeah. It'd be amaaaazing," Gem said. "Protips from Birdie B: 'We're going to celebrate Gem's *amaaaazing* performance.'"

She sounded so annoyed that Birdie actually stopped walking.

"Why'd you say it like that?" she asked Gem, who spun to face her on the sidewalk, her eyes still glittery with makeup.

"You don't think you were laying it on a little thick?" Gem asked. "When I saw you from the stage, I thought you wanted to be there, to support me. But you were crying because I got my wish first. Because everything's a competition with you."

"*Competition?*" Birdie said. "We're doing this together. And just now we needed an excuse to lose your parents! Also, I *do* think you were amazing. That's why I was crying! I wasn't laying anything on."

"Right," Gem said. You could spread her sarcasm with a knife.

Birdie threw down her bike. In typical Birdie fashion, she threw it down way too hard and definitely bent the frame, which meant she'd have to get out her dad's wrench again before her parents noticed and got mad. But she'd deal with that mess later. Right now, she had something she needed to get off her chest.

"Do you want to be friends anymore, Gem, or what?" Birdie put all her fears from the whole sucky sixth-grade year into the question.

"Of course I still want to be friends," Gem said without

missing a beat. She actually laughed, like this was ridiculous. "Birdie, we're always going to be friends."

The inside of Birdie's throat suddenly felt like it was being squeezed by a thousand hands. It made it hard to talk.

"You say that like it's obvious," she managed. "But I don't feel like we are friends anymore."

Gem looked away. She crossed her arms. Uncrossed them. She sighed. "It's because you're jealous of me."

"I am not!" Birdie sputtered. She couldn't believe Gem thought that. She looked at Marley, at Van—could they believe this?

"You're jealous," Gem went on, "that I granted my wish and you didn't."

"I'm proud of you!" Birdie shouted as a loud truck rumbled by. "Can't you tell the difference?" She was still shouting, even though the truck was gone around a corner. She heard herself, how loud she was.

Birdie breathed, like they said to do in those meditation videos Ms. Sae-Tang sometimes made them watch in English. She looked Gem in the eye and tried again.

"Sometimes my words come out bad. I know that. In my head, they're okay, but then . . . they make you so mad, Gem. I don't mean for them to."

Gem stared at her, chewing her lip. She didn't say anything, but it actually seemed like she was listening, so Birdie persevered.

"All I want is to have fun with you. To hang out with you. To make inside jokes with you. Like we used to. All I want is . . ."

There were twenty different endings to that sentence bouncing around Birdie's mind. Half of them would come out wrong. One was simple and true.

"All I want is you."

Gem started crying. Birdie couldn't tell if it was the good kind of crying or the bad kind of crying. She wanted to hug Gem, but she didn't have the confidence. She didn't have the confidence to hug her own best friend. Wow. Things had really gotten bad.

"I thought I could save her." Gem sniffed. "I thought my wish would be enough. This year has been so awful. I thought, if my wish were enough, it might make everything okay."

Birdie met Van and Marley's eyes again. She needed help. Van stepped forward, put their hand on Gem's back.

"We're on the same team," they said to Gem.

"No one expected you to do this alone," Marley added.

"If you could do it alone," Birdie finally found the words to say, "then what would you need us for?"

Gem wiped her eyes. She smiled at Birdie. "I need you for lots of things."

And that was when, out of the corner of Birdie's eye, she saw the black blur rushing toward them. She turned and there was Felix Howard on his skateboard, rolling fast in her direction.

"Butt-Ass has a stupid baby bag!" he shouted as he snatched the teddy bear backpack from Birdie's shoulder and tore off down the street.

THIRTY

Gem

Gem grabbed Birdie's bike with a guttural scream. She pedaled after Felix, heart ablaze. Something was wonky with the bike, but Gem couldn't let it stop her. She'd ride upside down through quicksand if it meant getting the fairy back safe.

Felix swung a left at the stop sign, causing an SUV to slam on its brakes and blare its horn. As he went around the corner, he glanced back and caught Gem's eye. He looked surprised to see her following.

She could hear Birdie and Marley shouting behind her, running to catch up. She heard the whizz of Van arriving at her side on their bike.

"He's heading for my da's neighborhood," Van shouted, pumping hard. "Come on."

Van took the lead as they tore down the street, away from the center of town. The sun blazed on Gem's shoulders as she swooped her arm over her head, beckoning Marley and Birdie to follow. They passed the sign for Oak Bluff, with its cheesy waterfall, then rode into the new development where half the houses were still under construction and all of them were huge.

Pickup trucks and portable dumpsters jutted out from every curb. Gem was glad for Van's help navigating.

"This way," they called, and pedaled faster.

The two of them trailed Felix, never gaining on him, and Gem wondered if Phoebe was scared. Gem's heart was pounding like it did in bad dreams.

Suddenly the skateboard turned, veering down a narrow alley. Gem lost sight of him, of the backpack. *Phoebe.* She pedaled harder. At last she reached the alley. It dead-ended in a pile of broken concrete, probably ten feet high. She didn't see Felix anywhere.

"Straight," Van said, and pedaled right up to the heap.

Gem did the same, then threw down the bike and started climbing. Hot sand and rubble filled her shoes. It was like climbing an avalanche; everything she tried to grab hold of crumbled downward, out of her grasp. It was slow-going and brutal, but somehow, eventually, with dirt in her hair and between her teeth, Gem made it to the top of the rubble. So had Van. They looked down from the summit into a yard with an empty swimming pool.

Felix was doing halfpipes on his skateboard in the pool. The bear bag was slung over his shoulder, as carelessly as if all it held was homework.

"Felix!" Gem's voice echoed off the sloped concrete walls. "Give us back that bag."

"Come down and make me, Cantaloupes," he taunted, still skating, not looking up.

"Careful what you wish for," Birdie panted, now at Gem's side.

"Well, if it isn't my old friend Butt-Ass," Felix said, squinting at Birdie, laughing his ugly laugh. "Oh, and Grandpa Joe," he called at Van, for reasons Gem couldn't understand. "And aw, the Little Loser," he said as Marley came to stand on the other side of Gem.

She linked her arm through her brother's.

"Go home, freaks," Felix shouted, doing an ollie. "Before I waste all of you."

"What does that even mean?" Birdie muttered.

Gem balled her fists. This was the moment when people backed down from Felix Howard. When his vague and stupid threats were just scary enough. This was when he'd burp in your face and claim victory.

Not today. Not with Phoebe at stake. Not when the four of them were together.

Gem took a step down the rubble. She slid a little, caught herself. The others started down with her, making their way to the empty pool. Until they were only a few feet away from Felix Howard. He stopped skating, his board still beneath his feet. He seemed to be trying to figure out what to do now that he hadn't scared them off.

He was bigger than all of them, and meaner. But he didn't want what was in the bag the way they did. And he didn't know, and he probably never would know, how to make a wish come true.

"You're just a bully," Gem said. "You say mean things and push people around and burp in everyone's face. And no one wants to be your friend. I bet that's lonely."

"You're fat—" he said, but his voice sounded wobbly, and Gem noticed he'd taken a step backward, off the skateboard. His eyes were wider than she'd seen them. Was he *scared*?

He was. It was the first time Gem realized that the four of them, together, were powerful.

"You're going to give us that bag and leave us alone," Gem said.

"You mean this bag?" His fingers moved toward the zipper.

Maybe he was nervous. In the scheme of schoolyard dynamics, that was huge. But a nervous bully could still hurt a fairy. Could still ruin everything.

"I wouldn't do that, Felix," Van said.

"Why not?" By then, Felix had opened the zipper all the way. He'd raised the bag up to his face and peered inside. His expression changed to disbelief.

"What the—"

Marley launched on top of Felix, knocking him over, onto his back. The bag thumped against the concrete, but it was still in Felix's hand. Gem winced, grabbing for it, trying to wrest it from Felix as her brother's fist reared back. Marley was just about to land the punch when Felix kneed him so hard Marley actually caught air. Her brother groaned, landing curled up a few feet away.

Before Felix could right himself, Phoebe flew out of the bag. She hovered a foot above his head. All of them stopped and stared. Her tiny body looked colorful and strong, but her wings were still dirty and damaged. It seemed to take an immense effort for her to fly, even a few feet in the air— but it was enough to freak Felix out.

"What is that, some kind of creepy drone?" he said, starting to back away, slow at first, then faster as Phoebe swooped closer, inches from Felix's face, like a bee.

Gem bet no one had dared get this close to the bully in a long time. She was afraid of what Felix might do, but he seemed almost paralyzed as Phoebe opened her mouth . . .

And let out a giant, reverberating belch.

It blew Felix's hair back. It made him flinch and cover his face. And then, when it should have ended, it didn't. It went on. And on.

At first, it sounded like a normal burp, only louder, longer—but then Gem realized there was more to the noise coming out of the fairy's mouth. Words? She listened closer. Nicknames. Insults. All the awful things Felix Howard said to everyone he encountered. All of it was . . . coming back at him. Phoebe was serving up a cacophony of hate and pain in gas form. Right in Felix Howard's face.

Gem glanced at Marley, who wore a cryptic smile, and suddenly she understood what was happening. *Marley's wish.* It was in the fairy's belly. It had been holding this revenge for Felix Howard all along.

The boy staggered backward. He crouched on his knees at the bottom of the empty pool. He looked shriveled up, in pain. As the fairy burp reached a crescendo, Gem heard her own nickname lobbed back at Felix. *Cantaloupes.*

Then the bully's eyes rolled back in his head and he fainted.

Phoebe closed her mouth. She let her wings flutter and she drifted to the ground. A silence followed. Then she turned to face the others and pressed a delicate hand to her lips.

"Excuse me," she said, and winked at Marley. "It must have been something I ate."

THIRTY-ONE

Birdie

Back at the crabapples, the kids caught their breath. It felt safer here than down in that empty pool, but Birdie was still on edge. Was she the only one still freaked? Van seemed all right, and Marley was grinning, triumphant. Phoebe too. Gem seemed to wear a new calm.

"See, Marley," Phoebe said, "it was an excellent wish after all."

"I keep thinking about Felix's expression," Gem said, climbing to sit on one of the low boughs of the tree. "Right before he passed out."

"What's he going to think when he wakes up?" Birdie wondered. "Will he remember?"

Phoebe gave Birdie a look that felt like a nudge. It took her a moment, but then—

"Oh, right," she said. "It'll be kind of like a dream."

"Now, where did we leave off before that unpleasant interruption?" Phoebe asked. "Birdie? Gem? You were saying?"

Birdie looked at her best friend, the glitter mixed with concrete dust on Gem's face, her new white sneakers trashed. A grown-up would say Gem needed a shower, but Birdie saw her differently—Gem looked brighter, happier, than she had in a long time. Birdie was glad for that, and also a little intimidated.

Birdie didn't want to go back and finish the fight they'd started on the street. But then she knew this was their pattern. All year she and Gem had been starting arguments they didn't finish, giving up midway because life interrupted, or one of them lost their nerve—usually Birdie. In the middle of their fights, Birdie sometimes feared the whole bottom of their friendship might drop out, and just be gone for good. She'd learned to cut off her anger like a water hose.

Was that why they kept having fights? Because they never really made up?

It was time to see what lay on the other side of the struggle. Birdie took a breath. She felt like an astronaut about to set foot on a new planet for the very first time.

"Sometimes, I wish we could go back to the way things were," she said. "Like last year. Like before that—"

"Well, we can't—" Gem said.

"I *know*—"

"But I wish we could too."

Birdie's head snapped up. Her eyes locked on Gem's. "Wait. You *do*?"

"Of course," Gem said. "Life used to be so much easier."

"Yeah!"

"You know, sometimes I'm jealous of you?"

"Get out of here," Birdie said, digging her toe in the dirt.

"You take everything in stride. You don't get all mad and hurt over dumb stuff like I do."

"I get mad and hurt."

Gem swallowed. "By me?"

"Sometimes."

There was a long quiet in the crabapples, wind rustling the leaves. Birdie felt like running away from her words. She felt like climbing to the top of the crabapples to get some space from the truth she'd just let out. She shouldn't have said it. Now Gem would—

"I'm sorry," Gem said, her voice a whisper. "I'm so sorry, Birdie."

"I'm sorry too." Birdie felt like she was choking on her truth. She wanted to say it, and it was so hard. This was *embarrassing*, and also, somehow, felt good.

"I have to tell you something," Birdie went on. "All of you. It's about my wish. It was to go to camp. But under that . . . that thing that was missing?"

"Yeah?" Gem said.

Birdie closed her eyes. "My wish was to not lose you, Gem."

She was crying by then, tears flowing like a mad river. She heard footsteps coming close, and she wanted to turn her back on them, but before she could, she smelled her best friend's lotus flower lotion, and Gem put her arms around Birdie and Birdie put her arms around Gem.

"You can't lose me," Gem said. She was crying now too. "We're going to change. Both of us. Maybe we'll become completely different people in five years. Or fifty. But I'm always going to want to be friends with you."

Birdie nodded into Gem's shoulder. She didn't have any more words. Gem had said them all. She hugged a little harder to let Gem know she got it.

That was when a sound came out of Birdie that she didn't expect to make. It was a thrilled kind of gasp as she felt warmth flood her body.

She knew this feeling. Had felt it before. Like she was being lifted up out of herself—

Her Granting.

Phoebe had drawn it out of her! Phoebe thought her wish was ready. Birdie put out her wrist. The pine charm hung on its golden chain. *Please work this time.*

The fairy guided the bracelet into the air to meet the halo of light. When the two parts of Birdie's wish touched, there was a beautiful golden spark. Like a little firecracker right before their eyes. Birdie saw herself at three years old, meeting teary-eyed Gem at the dentist. She saw a montage of a hundred sleepovers. She saw the afternoons doing homework at Gem's kitchen table. She saw Gem reading Birdie's first comic, cracking up. She saw them talking on the phone, Gem on her bed, Birdie holed up in her pantry. She saw them writing letters to each other in the summer when Gem was away at camp. She saw them fighting this past year. And fighting. And fighting. She saw Gem trying to throw Van off Birdie's back when the kid had tackled her that first day in the woods. She saw her face full of wonder watching Gem dance earlier today. Then she blinked and saw the real Gem standing right in front of her. Gem smiled. Birdie smiled.

Birdie felt . . . *granted.*

Golden light shot around the crabapples, like tiny birds set loose from a cage. Birdie laughed in awe as the sparks all slowly settled over Phoebe. Around her gray left wing.

It shimmered. It faded. Shimmered again. Then, with the suddenness of Christmas lights being turned on, Phoebe's wing burst into color—every color, all at once. It swelled and stretched and thickened until it was just the way Birdie remembered it from her long-ago dream.

"It's beautiful," she breathed.

"Thank you, Birdie," Phoebe said, making it flutter grandly, lighting up the crabapples with its luminescent glow.

Her wish had done this for Phoebe. Her wish made that wing a splendor.

It took Birdie a moment to see by contrast, the other wing—still pitiful and gray.

Birdie turned to Van.

THIRTY-TWO

Van

But how would they know if their wish was granted? Friendship wasn't something you could hold in your hand or see with your eyes. In certain moments these past few weeks, Van wondered if they'd made their wish come true already—but how could they prove it? How could they use it to heal Phoebe's wing?

"I don't know what to do," Van admitted.

"Tell them what you told me," Birdie said.

Van shook the chain to the base of their wrist so the small gold charm showed. "I thought the wish was about Caro, my friend from Ireland. But it's not. It's for friends who'll be as good as Caro was to me. Here. So I can feel at home."

"We're your friends, Van," Gem said, easy as a sunrise. Was that proof enough?

"Thanks." Their voice came out a whisper. They weren't the kind of kid who took friendship for granted. They turned to Phoebe, nervous to ask. "Would you try me?"

Phoebe turned to Van and put her hands out, as she'd done for Birdie and Gem. Van straightened, tried to make themself open, to be ready for whatever Phoebe needed. They waited to feel something. They closed their eyes and hoped. They pictured Mam back in Ireland as a girl, splashing through brooks and glens in search of fairies. They pictured Gran, ringing that bell to mark the fairy curfew. This was in Van's blood. They were connected to the fairy lore. They could help Phoebe. They could do this.

Nothing was happening. Van opened their eyes. Phoebe shook her head.

"I'm sorry. Not yet. There must be something underneath."

"Look what I found!" Marley called from beyond the crabapples. Van hadn't realized he'd left, but now he was threading his way back through the boughs. "It was with Dad's old stuff in the garage."

He held up a black plastic circle with red and green rings. A dartboard. And a Ziploc bag of plastic darts. And a hammer and a nail to tack it to the crabapple trunk.

"Marley," Gem said, "I'm sure Van's wish is more complex than just playing darts."

"Do you have a better idea?" he asked.

Van didn't. They took the board from Marley. It was plastic and battery-powered. When they used the hammer and nailed it to the tree, it wasn't anything like the antique corkboard in Caro's pub—but Van wondered if that was the point. After all, Phoebe wasn't anything like the fairies in fables back home. And Birdie and Gem and Marley weren't anything like Caro. Each were new facets of old things, sides previously unknown to Van.

They took a dart and stood back, focusing before they threw. They held their breath when the dart left their hand and let it out when they got a bull's-eye. This was not unheard of for Van's practiced arm—but still, a good sign.

"Let me try," Birdie said.

Van showed her how stand, how to hold her arm, when to breathe, and which angle to aim for at release. Birdie's dart hit the board, right next to Van's.

"Phoebe," Van said, holding out their hand. "Have a go. I'll hold you up." They lifted the fairy level to the board and pressed a dart into her hand.

"I'm too weak—"

"Give it a try," Van encouraged. "Otherwise you'll never know."

The fairy aimed. She focused. The dart sped past her

hand, but none of them saw where it landed, because—

"Look!" Gem gasped. She was pointing at Van.

"Van," Phoebe said, staring. "Your orb. You're doing it yourself."

"I am?" At first, Van couldn't see anything. They were overcome by a sensation of sureness in their chest. A bright burst of memories flashed before their eyes:

The first sight of Phoebe when they'd found her in the woods. Running Mam's sewing machine to make Gem's costume. Cheering for Marley as he wrested the backpack from Felix Howard. Leaving an anonymous comment on the school blog praising Birdie's comic, back before they'd ever spoken. And today—playing darts, nothing fancy, just showing the others what Van knew about the game. Their wish wasn't to *have* good friends in Texas. It was to *be* one. And they were.

"Oh," Van gasped as they saw their golden Granting hover before them.

Phoebe reached for Van's wrist, gently loosening the chain and its charm. They were surprised at how bare they felt without it, but then, they knew why: Theirs was the last wish. Granting it would mark an end. It would mean saying goodbye to Phoebe, sending her home.

Van watched as the orb absorbed their dart charm, as the light sparked around the crabapples. When the sparkling dust settled, Phoebe's wing was changing, color flowing through it. She was turning into someone who would leave them. She was becoming herself. Wondrous. Heartbreakingly wondrous.

"You did it," Birdie said, blubbering a sob.

"*We* did it," Van said, and squeezed her hand.

A previous Van would have to tried to hide that they were crying too. But not this Van, not today. Tears streamed down their face and they didn't even wipe them away.

"How are we going to say goodbye to you?" Marley said, a hitch in his voice.

"You're not. Not yet," Phoebe said.

"But what about Artemis? The Solstice and the Great Fire. Don't you have to go home and stop them?" Gem whispered.

Phoebe smiled. She hovered in the air before them now, flying easily, brilliantly, like she was meant to do. "Not until I grant one last wish." She winked. "My own."

"What is it?" Van asked. "What do you wish for?"

"Someone once told me not to tell anyone," Phoebe said. "Else it might not come true."

And then the fairy dipped her head and spread her wings so that they stretched wider than seemed possible, so that they spanned the crabapples. Van looked at the others. They knew what Phoebe wanted them to do.

"Can you hold us all?" Van asked.

"Have a little faith," the fairy said.

They climbed atop the fairy's wings. Gem and Marley on her left side, Birdie and Van on her right. They sunk their fingers into plush, dense, magic wings and hung on as the fairy took flight. Birdie and Marley whooped. Gem screamed with glee. Van's pleasure stuck in their throat as they shot up and out of the top of the crabapples.

Into sudden sunlight. Into sky-blue air. Van looked up, and down, and all around. They couldn't believe how right it felt to fly.

"Look!" Gem pointed. There was her and Marley's house, growing smaller. And there, the woods where the fairy first fell. There was Van's da's neighborhood, his swimming pool and diving board. There, the empty pool down the street, where they'd faced down Felix Howard. There was Wonder Middle School, holding unknown seventh-grade secrets. There was the street where Birdie's and Van's homes stood on opposite sides. There was the highway that led out of town—and Dallas, far in the distance. Van closed their eyes and imagined Ireland, farther still. For once it didn't hurt to think of Ireland. For once, they were glad to be right here. Wind rippled their hair. Sun danced on their skin. The world grew brighter, dazzlingly bright, until Van couldn't see anything, and then—

The crabapples. Van was sitting inside them, perched on their favorite bough. Birdie was one bough up, kicking

Van's shoulder absently with her shoe. Marley was crouched on his knees, checking out a giant mushroom that had sprung up at the base of the trunk. Gem lay on her back, gazing at blue sky through branches.

"How long have we been here?" Birdie asked, sounding dazed.

"I don't know," Gem said.

"It's so hot," Marley said. "I can't stand it."

"Y'all should come over," Van said, like it was the simplest thing in the world. And maybe it was. "My da's got a pool."

ACKNOWLEDGMENTS

With thanks to Laura Rennert, fairy fortress of support. To Reka Simonsen, who perceived the fairy highway to this book's completion. To the fairy clan at Atheneum for translating a glimmer into a book, and for a cover that resembles my childhood sanctuary. To Boon Goetsh and Raya Bloom, wise and early seers. To Kris Armetta, on every page. To Megan Bloom, my best Gem. To Jason, goblin of love. To Matilda, who knew they had to save the fairy. And to Venice, for his faith, clear as silver bells.